ANDRE GONZALEZ

Time of Fate

For Felix. See something through its end, and you'll be surprised how much you've achieved.

"Time is a drug. Too much of it kills you."

-Terry Pratchett

Contents

GET EXCLUSIVE BONUS STORIES!

Connecting with readers is the best part of this job. Releasing a book into the world is a truly frightening moment every time it happens! Hearing your feedback, whether good or bad, goes a long in shaping future projects and helping me grow as a writer. I also like to take readers behind the scenes on occasion and share what is happening in my wild world of writing. If you're interested, please consider joining my mailing list. If you do so, I'll send you the following as a thank you:

1. A free copy of *Revolution,* a prequel story that goes back in time before Chris Speidel ever knew about the mysterious world of time travel.
2. A free copy of *Road Runners,* a prequel story that visits the origination of the Road Runners organization.

You can get your content **for free,** by signing up HERE.
https://www.andregonzalez.net/Wealth-Of-Time-Bonus

Chapter 1

Martin Briar leaned back on the couch, a glass of moonshine resting on the coffee table in front of him. He and his team had spent the last two weeks living in the same apartment building as Sonya Griffiths, plotting to either capture or kill her, ready to advance to the final stages of ending Chris Speidel's life. He had admitted to his team, in the early days of their arrival, that his decision to fly out to 1933 Chicago was a knee-jerk reaction.

In a matter of weeks as the newly elected commander, Martin had endured the attacks on their Las Vegas hotel, treason from Councilwoman Murray, and the death of his lieutenant commander, Gerald Holmes. All orchestrated by Chris and the Revolution, and their sister organization of disgruntled Road Runners, the Liberation.

Yes, the goal had always been to capture Chris, but the urgency intensified once Gerald was murdered on Chris's Idaho property.

"I can't believe tomorrow is the big day," Martin said, leaning forward to take a sip from his glass. The planning was done, and hardly any of it focused on their actual attempt to break into Sonya's apartment. That part was straightforward: knock on her door with hopes of baiting her with a peaceful discussion, or if not, kicking the door down and barging in to

1

take her. Either way, Martin *was* getting into that apartment. The plans they had formulated centered on what to do if Sonya decided to run. She had a new bottle of Juice and could slip away to a different era with a quick swig. The Road Runners had teams planted all throughout time at this specific location, ready for Sonya to appear.

Extensive research went into this matter, analyzing the trends of where Sonya liked to time travel, eliminating anything before the 1400s and after the year 2100. Seven hundred years was plenty of territory to cover, but they only required two Road Runners per year. While Sonya could travel to a specific date of her choosing, they presumed—and hoped—that she would rush her decision and request only a specific year, prompting the rules of time travel to transport her to the same exact day and time in a different year.

"We're ready for whatever happens," said the new lieutenant commander, Alina Herrera. "All possible outcomes are accounted for—we just need to execute and react." Alina had spent every day in her new role plotting the eventual death of Chris Speidel, but had joined the crew in Chicago two days ago to review their plans and look for any vulnerabilities. Alina had been a Road Runner for over a decade, running missions in Central America to stop violence from the same drug cartels that had taken her father's life in front her own eyes as a six-year-old girl.

She sat in one of two lounge chairs across from Martin, the other occupied by their top agent, Arielle Lucila. Between Arielle and Alina, Martin had two of the most talented minds and agents that the organization had to offer. Alina would stay back while Martin encountered Sonya, needing to remain safe in case Martin died, but Arielle planned to wait directly outside

Sonya's apartment.

They both had pistols lying on the coffee table. Alina smoked a cigarette in place of a drink, while Arielle opted to chew gum to settle her nerves.

"I want to thank you both," Martin said. "Arielle, you whipped together this team so fast and have shown how forward-thinking you are with all of this planning. Your attention to detail is unlike anything I've seen before. And Alina, I know that if everything works out we'll have a clear, simple path to finally getting rid of Chris. Cheers to you both."

Martin raised his drink before gulping down its remains and slamming the glass on the table.

"We're honored to just be working on this mission," Arielle said with a grin, brushing back her honey-brown hair. "In our line of work, even with how dangerous it is, so many of the missions can feel repetitive. Our days sort of blend together: fight the bad guys, save the innocents, you know? But this has breathed new life into me. I don't think I've been this excited to be a Road Runner since I first joined."

Alina nodded in agreement. "It's true, Commander. There are so many of us working hard every day, knowing it's for the greater good. I never dreamt in a million years that I would one day serve as lieutenant commander."

Martin shrugged. "I don't know what to say—I was elected into a job I didn't really want or know how to do. All I wanted was to surround myself with the best talent, and that has led to you two, which has led to your teams that are here with us. My only goal is to kill Chris. Once that's done, we can return to the days of doing meaningful missions—all of us. I want everyone in this organization to feel empowered to do their best work and move their lives in the directions they want. And that starts from the top down. If this is successful, you can both do whatever you want, as far as I'm concerned. Arielle, if you want to be a Lead Runner, just tell me where. Alina, you're stuck with me for a couple years, but after that, you'll have my full endorsement for the commandership, should you like."

Alina smiled. "I appreciate that, Commander, but let's worry about one thing at a time and get Sonya tomorrow."

"Of course," Martin said. "I'd be lying if I told you I wasn't thinking about my own death—it's certainly more than possible tomorrow. That's why I wanted to thank you both, just in case."

"And that's where we're different, Commander," Arielle said. "You see, we don't have that mentality. We're aware that death is possible every mission, but we don't dwell on it. We are the better team in this battle, and you must always remember that."

Martin nodded. "Thank you for that."

"We should probably call it a night," Arielle said, checking her watch. The evening had crept past nine o'clock, a potential long night of tossing and turning ahead. Arielle and Alina both stood, prompting Martin to follow suit. They shared an apartment unit four doors down the hallway. The entire team was spread all over the complex, able to snag units for dirt cheap, considering they were in the Great Depression.

Sonya lived on the third floor, an advantage for the Road Runners, as they could jam the stairwells should she try to flee her apartment. She wouldn't make it off her floor before a flock of Road Runners swarmed her.

"Sleep well, Commander," Alina said. "I'm gonna look everything over one final time before going to bed—can never be too sure."

4

"And I'll try to fall asleep and fail miserably," Arielle said. "Been that way my whole life—I'm a night owl at heart. Must be why it's so hard for me to get out of bed in the mornings."

Martin chuckled. "Learning what makes you two tick these last couple weeks has been really interesting. I'll be asleep in two minutes—the moonshine has that effect."

"I could go into the science of why that stuff is absolutely horrible for you, but I know you won't actually care," Arielle said, letting out a light giggle.

"I've been drinking alcohol my whole life," Martin said. "This stuff may not taste the best, but it serves its purpose. Now, you ladies have a good night, and I'll see you in the morning."

"Good night, Commander," Arielle said, leading the way out.

Martin closed the door, falling back into the silence of isolation. He poured one more glass of moonshine to polish off before calling it a day. The stress had mounted to unprecedented levels. Aside from this two-week mission, he still had daily responsibilities to tend to: putting out small fires around the continent, approving and denying special mission requests, and attempting to remain a transparent and accessible commander for the organization.

The silence was nothing but a double-edged sword. He enjoyed the time to himself to unwind and not constantly live in the bustle, but it also prompted his mind to churn out wild thoughts and scenarios. Maybe Sonya would want to run away with him forever, disappearing into the sunset where they'd build new lives together. The future tormented him.

Martin returned to the couch with his full glass, sinking into it as he pulled out his wallet, flipping it open to the old, tattered photo he kept of his late daughter, Izzy. He ran a thumb over its plastic covering, her adolescent grin wide and cheerful. "I don't know if this all happened because of you. Maybe I've just been telling myself that to keep my heart in it. Worst-case scenario, I'll be seeing you soon. Best case, I'm a hero."

Martin turned on the radio, still not quite used to having that as the only means of in-home entertainment, and listened to a jazz station while he finished off his nightcap, eventually falling into a deep sleep on the couch for his final night in 1933.

Chapter 2

Duane and Chris sat in Wealth of Time's back office in the northern Nevada desert. Beautiful, unincorporated territory, as Chris liked to refer to it.

Chris had listened to Duane spew for the past hour about the pending doom awaiting the Revolution. A natural optimist toward his beloved Revolters, Chris dismissed Duane's warnings. Duane also admitted that he'd been pondering the relevance of the Revolution ever since his mother's final days had ended in such turmoil.

He referred to it as a true eye-opening experience in his life, his very own coming-to-Jesus moment. Chris balked, calling Duane *soft* and *emotional.* The Revolution had long been carved out for unchecked masculinity, and Chris tolerated nothing less.

"I have nothing but respect for you, Chris," Duane said, eyes gloomy as they locked on the Keeper of Time. "And that's why I'm telling you—just like when my mom got sick—that my heart isn't in this right now. Out of my love to the Revolution, I owe it to inform you of this. We need a strong, synchronized leadership, and I can't commit to that right now."

Chris had sensed the doom, but would never admit it. The pillars of the Revolution had cracked and collapsed one at a time, Duane's departure perhaps the final, fatal blow.

"I can't say I recall the sensation of having such human feelings," Chris said. "But if I may, you sound like you only want to quit because of our predicament. You're jumping ship."

"No. It's the classic tale of 'it's not you, it's me.' I want the Road Runners executed—I just can't be a part of that moment. If my head's not in it, then my heart's not in it, and that's just as destructive."

"I've been betrayed so many times during my reign," Chris said. "Every bone in my body knows I can trust you with anything, but there's a chance this is a ploy. It's always a shock, and never from someone I'd expect. I suppose those most loyal to you have the most to gain from witnessing—or enabling—your downfall."

"You know better than that," Duane said in his usual calm tone. "I love this organization and would never betray it."

Chris leaned back and nodded. "I'm not in a position to find a new number two right now, especially because you want to go dancing on the beach somewhere—it's not a good reason."

"My reason doesn't matter—I'm being upfront and honest with you. I can't commit to the organization right now. That's not to say I'm leaving forever – I guess you could call this an indefinite leave of absence."

Chris shook his head. "I can't do this without you. You think of the things I don't, make the detailed plans for so many things on a daily basis."

"You've never *needed* me. Anyone can do the things I do, except for presenting you with different perspectives. But that's also why I feel like now is the time for me to step away—there are no more decisions to make. All roads point to a showdown between you and Martin, and nothing is going to change that fate. You can plan all the attacks you want on the Road Runners; it's only going to speed up that process. You should be throwing everything to the wind and focusing solely on how you plan to counter Martin when he shows up for you."

"Oh, please, I'm not afraid of Martin Briar. He has a mere fraction of my abilities, a dance with him only ends in his death."

"We both know that's a lie. You may not be afraid, per se, but you're worried. No attacks have been authorized, recruiting efforts have been ramped up. You're playing defense, and I know that, but that doesn't mean the Road Runners do."

"The war doesn't *feel* like it's moving toward an end. No one has attacked in two weeks. What do you suppose that means?" He knew Duane was leaving tonight, and needed to milk the last bits of information he could from his lifelong confidant.

"They're plotting. We watch their newsfeed. They used to have a weekly segment where the commander addresses the organization and fields questions—that hasn't happened in two weeks. The regular news broadcast usually discusses the happenings of the leadership team once or twice a day—that hasn't happened in two weeks, either. They're planning something, and will come out swinging."

"I fear no man, but I'll admit I regret recruiting Briar. We don't look into the future for all of our recruits, but maybe we should. Briar inspired a movement with his zero to hero story, and that's my fault for ever letting it reach this point. We should have stayed in his house after killing his mom, and taken him. They would have picked an established Road Runner to run for commander, and all would be the same today."

"It's impossible to do a thorough deep-dive into all recruits. Less than one percent of new recruits come through your office;

it's all so widespread. We grew without ever implementing a consistent recruitment process or standards."

Duane had mentioned this several times, but Chris didn't care. He just wanted as many bodies in his organization as possible, happy to deal with any troublemakers along the way.

"There's something else you should know before I leave," Duane said.

"That you were kidding, right? This is a big joke?"

"No, Chris, this is serious, and I had held off on telling you with hopes of the news fizzling away. You don't have time to deal with this, but I suppose no one else can."

"Spit it out."

"I'm in many meetings and hear lots of things. It's been mentioned that the Liberation is making plans of their own to overthrow you."

Chris threw his head back and laughed. "That's precious—they have no means of pulling off such a feat. I like Thaddeus, and he likes me. I think he'd be the natural fit to replace you."

Duane shook his head harshly. "Under no circumstances should you do that. It's time to cut your ties with the Liberation and consider them an enemy just as dangerous as the Road Runners."

"But they hate the Road Runners."

"Well, they hate you too."

"I've never had so much as a disagreement with Thad since we started working together."

"He's playing you, Chris. I'm not sure if it's been his plan all along, but it is now."

"Why would anyone discuss this in front of you? I don't understand."

"It wasn't directly discussed in front of me, but I caught wind of it and fact-checked it myself. It all makes sense. Haven't you noticed the Liberation has also gone quiet?"

"Well, no, because they take orders from myself and Thaddeus. We chat once a week and last he told me, they were working on replenishing their supplies and outlining new strategies for future arson missions. Sounds to me they're ready to get back to work."

"I know once I leave this room you'll believe me. I have no reason to make this up. Tread carefully, and keep this in mind during your future conversations with Thaddeus. He might start asking questions about your schedule and whereabouts—they're planning a coup and want to hijack the Revolution and all of its resources. You're the only one in the way of making that happen."

Chris smirked. "I believe it, even if I haven't seen it for myself. It's a shame. I actually liked the work they were doing at the Liberation, but now I'll have to remove them from existence just like all the other small groups that formed in the past."

"You have the experience in these matters; taking them out should be a cakewalk. I really need to get going now, though."

Duane stood, his lips pursed as he waited for Chris to join him.

"So just like that, it's over?" Chris asked. "Nearly fifty years—in real time—of work down the drain, leaving me to fend for myself in a fistfight with Martin Briar. *Thousands* of years if you add it all up."

"Why do you act like you've never been in this position before? I can think of five right off the top of my head, and each instance you came out on top. You're still invincible. What are you worried about?"

Chris worried about plenty. Martin could authorize time be frozen and resist it, leaving all Revolution soldiers useless, and a one-on-one battle between the two leaders. He also had a standing appointment for a phone call with Sonya every Monday, one that she had to initiate since she was living in 1933. A lot could happen to her within seven days—the unknowing made him paranoid. He gave her his word that he'd leave her alone, and he had so far. The last thing anyone would call Chris Speidel was a liar, but it might be time to renegotiate their terms. His life was on the line, and whether Sonya cared or not didn't change that fact.

"I'm not worried," Chris said again, more to assure himself. Once Duane left, it was true that nothing would change. He'd still be in the same predicament, and if Martin froze time it would deem Duane irrelevant anyway. He was on his own, and surely Martin understood this simple fact. "I know it'll be fine, but can't you agree that something feels *different* this time around?"

Duane shrugged, slipping on his coat. "Sure, because Martin can somewhat level the playing field, but remember—he'll still be on his own. If it comes down to it and you need to run, you know all the hidden trap doors this continent has to offer."

"The day I hide from a Road Runner is the day I die," Chris snapped. "You speak like they have Sonya in their possession."

"Sonya's fine. She doesn't want to get tangled in this mess any more than you do. She's done picking sides and just wants to live her life—there's nothing you or Martin can say to change that. The Liberation has been searching for her, but they're nowhere close. They don't have the access to information like we do—they're essentially throwing darts at a board. Blindly, at best."

Duane picked up the lone suitcase of his few belongings, and started toward the front door.

"Goodbye, my friend," Chris said. "I do hope you'll reconsider staying, or coming back sooner."

"I wouldn't count on that, Chris. I wish you the best. I'll be watching from afar, but I know you'll be just fine."

Chris stuck out a hand, growing thinner and bonier by the day. He knew his body would keep aging no matter what he did, but he didn't care. He was strong despite his deteriorating appearance—his mind still sharp, his soul as hungry as ever to exterminate Road Runners.

"Thank you for everything. This organization wouldn't be where it is without you. Don't be a stranger."

"I wouldn't dream of it—I'll be in touch."

With that, Duane Betts walked out of the house and out of Chris's life forever, never to speak another word to the Keeper of Time.

Chapter 3

Martin enforced that no one was to leave the apartment complex without his approval. Even a trip to the grocery store was off limits, so they had each packed additional suitcases of all the food they needed, sure to never be spotted by Sonya.

On the morning of another winter Chicago day in 1933, Martin sat at his kitchen table with an opened Pop-Tart wrapper, crumbs scattered next to a steaming mug of tea. He had no consistent diet since arriving to the Great Depression, but it didn't matter. All he wanted was to either kill Sonya Griffiths or convince her to return to the Road Runners and assist with the capture of her father.

Nerves bubbled in his stomach, each bite of the artificial strawberry flavoring a chore to force down. The tea made his head spin, too hot for such a rattled state of mind. His own potential death consumed his thoughts, and pushing them away was near impossible.

Sitting at the table reminded him of the time he had confessed to his mother about his participation in this world of time travel, back in 2019 at the kitchen table in their Littleton mansion. He had expected an argument over the validity of his claims, but all Marilyn did was encourage him to see this adventure through its end.

"So what if you die? Everyone dies at some point." He whispered her words, the weight of each one pressing against his skull. He had no plans of dying, but that matter wasn't up to him.

A knock banged on the door, startling Martin as he nearly fumbled the mug. "Alina?" he called, expecting his lieutenant to stop by before the plans moved forward.

"Yes, sir," her muffled voice replied from the other side.

Martin rose and trudged across the apartment to let her in. She wore their official combat uniform, navy blue spandex material with thick padding covering the entire torso. While she wasn't involved in the mission, she wanted to remain prepared in case she had to intervene at any point. Mainly, the uniform provided the best flexibility for running long distances or engaging in close combat.

"Good morning, Commander," she greeted, her black hair twisted into a braid. "Are you ready to execute this mission in twenty-seven minutes?" She checked her watch to confirm the precise time.

"No time like the present," Martin said, offering a forced grin.

"Good. Everyone will be moving into their positions in exactly twelve minutes. From there, we wait for you. Have you tested your radio again this morning?"

They had brought radios from the future, technology a hit-or-miss while traveling throughout time, depending on which technologies existed in the era.

"Still works. I paged Arielle to test. And have you notified the Council of our plans today?"

"Yes. The Council has been alerted that you are ready to head in—they wish you the best of luck."

"Did they really?" Martin asked, rolling his eyes. He and the

15

Council had gotten into several heated arguments regarding his decision to take on this mission firsthand. They didn't mind him scouting the area and staying in 1933 to make plans for capturing Sonya, but the moment he declared that he'd be the one barging into her apartment, Chief Councilman Uribe brought their operations to an immediate halt.

Uribe had called it reckless and irresponsible. The organization had already been through enough over the past several months, and there was no reason for their leader to once again be placed in serious jeopardy. He brought the issue to a formal vote on three different occasions, a 4 to 3 count returning each time in favor of letting the commander do as he saw fit, Martin forever grateful for having stacked the Council in his favor.

Those opposed, including Uribe, took a deep dive into the Road Runner Bylaws, throwing every rule they could at Martin and their fellow Councilors to stop it from happening. Nothing resisted the power of their votes, and it was settled that Martin would carry out the mission.

The Council eventually pleaded with Commander Blair in Europe to help by freezing time, but Martin's British counterpart was still pissed Gerald had been killed in what he deemed a "sloppy mission that should have never happened." He vowed to not offer any more assistance with Martin's antics in trying to kill Chris. From his point of view, the war in North America was bad, yes, but not something that warranted such desperate moves. He did not give his blessing for Martin to enter the mission on his own, but Martin didn't give a shit.

"They did," Alina said, stepping all the way into the apartment, taking a seat at the kitchen table. Martin made his way to the couch he had passed out on last night. "I traveled ahead and spoke to Uribe—he really does wish you the best and said he can't wait to speak with you in person."

Martin grinned. "I know things got ugly, but he's a phenomenal man."

"That he is." Alina checked her watch again, something she had been doing just about every minute. She was much more organized than Martin, an attribute desperately needed for their leadership team. Every meeting was prompt with its start and end times, Alina having too much to focus on to get dragged into wasted time.

On her first day as the new lieutenant, she stood up and left Martin's office in the middle of a conversation, citing that her next time block was due for research on places to stash Chris's dead body. Martin had been taken aback when this happened, but had since learned to appreciate her dedication in the days since. He might have been the one doing the dirty work in capturing Sonya, but Alina would ensure none of their efforts went down the drain.

"Everything is in place should you not make it back," Alina said. "Your will has been sent to the Council for safety, and our elections team has made preliminary preparations in case both of us don't make it for some reason. All bases are covered, including the flip side for what will happen if Sonya is killed, captured, or escapes."

"Perfect, thank you. Should we start getting ready to head out there?" Martin asked, the words making his head spin.

"Yes."

Martin pulled himself off the couch and opened the closet door in the short hallway that led to his bedroom. He slipped into an armored vest and helmet, having opted to not wear a combat uniform since his role was confined to Sonya's apartment. If she ran, everyone else on the team was ready

17

to chase.

If they had prepared him like this for his first attempt on Sonya's life in 1996, he wondered if things would have played out any differently. He never planned to kill her during that initial visit, but things had since changed.

He grabbed a loaded pistol and slipped it into his utility belt, already equipped with pepper spray and a taser. Martin had no intention of using any of these weapons, considering them more as tools of self-defense. Sonya would dictate how this encounter played out, Martin wanting a peaceful discussion where they could explore all available options.

"Three minutes," Alina informed him. "You should start heading up." She brought him the radio he had left on the kitchen table, sticking it in his hand.

Martin nodded and took a deep breath. "I'll see you on the other side, Lieutenant."

Alina stuck out a hand to shake, Martin grabbing it firmly. "I know you'll do great."

They left his apartment together, reaching the stairwell where Alina went down to her first floor apartment, and Martin took the flight up to the third floor where Sonya waited. He hadn't been on the third floor since their first day living in the complex, and had only seen photographs and diagrams of the floor during their intensive planning. He checked his watch to find one minute remaining until he was expected to knock on her door.

His legs dragged down the hallway, thoughts swirling out of control as his breathing elevated to a much faster pace. Martin had put on a pair of gloves, anticipating the nervous sweat that always seemed to accompany him during moments of anxiety. He needed to grip his weapons if it came to it. The body armor felt like an elephant on his back.

Unit 312 had a slightly crooked door in the middle of the long hallway, and Martin drew one more deep breath when he reached it, hand trembling as he raised it and knocked. He took a step back and raised his hands in the air to show there was no harm intended, waiting to see if Sonya would answer.

Chapter 4

The grand mission to rid the world of Chris Speidel had many moving parts. While one team worked in 1933 Chicago, another remained in 2020 northern Nevada, a mere ten-minute helicopter ride away from the Wealth of Time storefront. Arielle Lucila, who went on the Chicago trip, had planned the pending attack on the store and served as a liaison between the two teams.

They didn't want one event to occur without the other, so when Arielle called thirty minutes ago giving the green light, confirming that all was in place in Chicago, a grin came to the lips of Justin Fowler, a longtime Road Runner and current Lead Runner of the nearby Salt Lake City office.

He and Arielle had formed this team together, finding the best twenty soldiers available in North America. They had arrived by helicopter two days earlier, setting up tents as they made final preparations for what was to be a first-time mission for the Road Runners: dropping bombs on a Revolution hideout.

While the Road Runners kept a plethora of explosives, they had only ever used them when they blew up Chris's Alaskan mansion. Never had they dropped bombs from above, but this was a unique opportunity thanks to the severely remote location of the store.

Besides, no commander had ever legally authorized the use of bombs until Briar, bringing with him a ruthless approach the organization had never seen before. He spared no expense or efforts in his lone goal of bringing down Chris. Some soldiers on the team speculated that Commander Briar was letting the organization run on autopilot—as rarely making appearances and giving updates became custom. But no one let that fact bother them, as they witnessed a refreshing, serious approach to bring down the Keeper of Time.

"Balls to the walls," Justin told his team, a collection of equally ruthless men and women with an insatiable hunger to kill Revolters. "This is Commander Briar's approach, and it will be ours this morning. Are there any last questions before we head over?"

He looked to the huddle of blank faces, many concealed behind face coverings as part of their combat attire. The soldiers dressed in their uniforms, helmets on, rifles loaded. An all-out raid was on the menu, and not a single one of them wanted to back down now.

Justin declared it time to proceed. They broke into groups and dispersed in different directions, Justin heading to the chopper equipped with the explosives. Four soldiers joined him, including the pilot, while the other sixteen packed into three different trucks that would arrive to the scene seconds after the explosions started. The intent behind the bombs was not to kill those inside, but to destroy the building—a beautiful, symbolic gesture according to Commander Briar, who had explained all of his troubles with Chris had stemmed from that very edifice.

Once the structure absorbed its damage, those inside would have no choice but to run out where they'd meet the gunfire of those soldiers in the trucks. Commander Briar told them to be ready for anything, including large numbers of Revolters. He cited the time he and Gerald had wanted to stop by, but several cars had appeared in the parking lot after a week of surveillance suggested otherwise. He suspected the store was being used as a hub to funnel Revolters from all around the sphere of time, meaning it was impossible to know their true numbers. That was another reason he justified the bombs, Gerald having instilled the strategy of putting enemies on defense and catching them off guard.

Timing was everything on this mission, an attribute that separated the great soldiers from the elite. The helicopter had been started, leaving them exactly five minutes until take off. Justin and the rest of his crew filed in, he taking the co-pilot seat where he'd make the decision to deploy the bombs.

They all slipped on a pair of headsets as the engine and rotor drowned out any possibility of normal conversation. The pilot entered last, a large man by the name of Sergio Fritteli, who seemed to rock the entire chopper as he made his way to the pilot's seat.

"Everyone ready to roll?" he asked through the headset.

Justin gave a thumbs up while the other two in the back whooped and hollered like rowdy high schoolers. This earned a satisfied chuckle from Sergio, who started flipping switches on the dashboard. "One minute until takeoff," he said, the vibrations growing stronger, a sense of destiny sprinkling over the nerves starting to form in Justin's gut.

"Balls to the walls!" Justin shouted as he looked out his window to the rest of the group already in their trucks, a few hanging out the backseat windows for a better view of the road ahead. He had encouraged them to watch the show, to embrace being part of the most important history for the Road Runners.

"Off we go!" Sergio cried, the helicopter beginning its ascent. They climbed in altitude, not needing to go much higher than 300 feet for this trip, but Justin caught a breathtaking view of the desert. Every way he looked was sheer golden sand, daunting with its isolation, but welcoming with its guaranteed privacy at the same time.

Wealth of Time stood tall and sturdy, about the size of the old Target stores before they all turned into supercenters. Justin had never seen it for himself until this mission, and this elevated angle provided him a glimpse of its grandness. He couldn't wait to demolish it.

They started moving forward, and within seconds had left the trucks behind, where they'd soon start the drive over.

"We're taking it slow," Justin said. "Let's keep our eyes on the property, but give time for the trucks to get over there."

Sergio already knew this and shot a thumb up to Justin. "Roger that."

Justin grabbed his binoculars and looked out the window to the world below, pleased to find the trucks had already taken off, set to drive at a clip above 100 miles per hour. All they needed was a three-minute head-start, but Arielle had suggested they wait to leave until the helicopter got in the air, just in case they ran into any mechanical difficulties upon takeoff.

Those three minutes suspended in the air dragged for Justin, and surely all of those inside. He passed the time by watching the trucks move below, clouds of dust following behind their small caravan. He stole a glance to the store, undisturbed under the beaming sun. They had discussed what to do if the people inside heard the helicopter ahead of time and headed outside. Justin declared that shouldn't make a difference in

23

their approach—they still had to destroy the building. Surely nothing the Revolters had on the ground could deter that from happening.

"We're clear," Sergio said, having kept track of the three-minute interval himself, and started forward.

Justin put the binoculars on his lap and watched ahead, the store growing bigger with each passing second. He had half expected retaliation. Surely Chris had strengthened his security at his offices and buildings around the continent after his mansion went up in flames. But that wasn't the case, nor would it ever be, seeing as Chris was invincible and didn't give an actual shit about those who worked for him. Perhaps he believed the Road Runners would never follow through with another air assault after their last one failed under Julian Caruso, a gamble Commander Briar had won.

It's not supposed to be this easy, Justin thought. But it was. It only took them seven minutes to reach the point of no return, inching closer to once again turning the Revolution on its side.

Doubt crept into his thoughts. Did Chris have a way of knowing all of this was coming his way, yet allowed the Road Runners to carry out their plans as a way of ambushing them in a twisted trap? It didn't seem so far-fetched considering Chris's history of mind games, possibly even likely.

Another topic that had been discussed but not truly addressed was the building itself. A handful of those on the team had shared their experiences of entering Wealth of Time, all in different cities at different times. How did they know the store standing in the desert was real, especially in the middle of an area known for mirages? Theories spun out of control during their initial discussion, and it was pushed to the back burner as something they would try to extract from Sonya once they captured her. Some believed the store itself was a portal for time travel, or that it was built above a supernatural energy source. If this same desert housed the supposed aliens in Area 51 hundreds of miles south, then what else could be possible?

Despite all the doubt, no resistance met them as Sergio said, "We're now in range to hit the store."

Justin took one final peek through the binoculars, finding no one outside, no secret doors with machine guns pointing up at them. Just a massive wooden structure ready to meet its death. He looked to Sergio, whose hands had come off the control wheel to flip new switches, and promptly returned to start aiming their ammunition.

"Knock that piece of shit down!" Justin barked, suddenly overcome with euphoria as he realized this was indeed falling into place without interruption. The airwaves through the headsets fell silent as the helicopter rumbled violently, a trail of smoke zooming to the store ahead, trailing its missile.

The first one hit the eastern side of the building and sent a fiery orange cloud into the sky, chunks of wooden shrapnel flying in every direction. Sergio deployed the next, followed by two more, all within twenty seconds.

Between the smoke trails and explosions below, visibility had momentarily been eliminated, prompting Sergio to descend through the black clouds of ash. They had already planned on touching down and joining the festivities, and once they cleared the smoke, found the rest of the team pulling up in the trucks, jumping out and immediately opening fire.

The store looked like a tornado had just pummeled it, piles of splintered wood and drywall standing in smoldering stacks while smoke oozed from the rubble. A handful of people scampered from the store's remains, promptly greeted by a shower of bullets.

Sergio continued to lower the helicopter and they touched the ground within minutes, the blades swirling dust in every direction, their blaring sound drowning out the rapid gunfire that took life after life.

Six bodies already lay on the ground, a few twitching as they clung to their last breaths. Three more rose from the rubble and darted away from the building, meeting the same fate as their friends before.

"I need to find Mario Webster," Justin said. "We believe he is the highest-ranking Revolter at this location." Sergio stood from the cockpit and opened the door, waving an arm for Justin to exit. He cocked his pistol before climbing down, but knew he wouldn't need it—his team had everything under control.

He jogged toward the commotion, the gunfire having ceased now that no one else was dashing from the crumbled remains of the store. If they hadn't caught a bullet, they were certainly suffocating under the debris. The thought drew a smile.

The bodies lay scattered about the desert ground, and the first one Justin approached was already dead. But it wasn't Mario. He checked the two nearest, finding one with a face smeared in blood and soot, another gurgling on his own blood while gazing blankly to the sky, not even *seeing* Justin over him. Neither man was Mario, so he moved on to the next body and found his guy.

"Mr. Webster," Justin said with a grin, waving to the others waiting nearby. They had instructions to clear the bodies from the scene by tossing them into the rubble which would soon be doused with kerosene for a final cremation of the store's remains.

"You motherfuckers," Mario said through gritted teeth, his

strong voice catching Justin off guard. He writhed on the ground, blood streaming from his left arm and right leg.

"Lucky man," Justin said, squatting beside Mario's wounded arm, knowing he had no strength to make a move on him. "You catch two bullets and not one seems to have sliced through an organ or artery. Maybe we'll pack you in a box and drop you at the doorstep in Idaho. How does that sound?"

Mario smiled, his teeth shiny against his ashy skin. "You're fucked. You just signed the death warrants for all of your people here. Do you really think Chris is going to turn the cheek after you blew up his most prized building?"

Justin reared back a fist and slammed it into Mario's left temple, earning a satisfying groan as his head bobbed from side to side. He knelt closer to Mario, lowering his lips within an inch of his ear. "I don't give a *shit* about Chris," he said. "Your old man is on his last leg. Do *you* think we would knock this building down for fun? The end of this war is coming, and there's nothing you can do to stop it."

Mario rolled his head back to meet Justin's eyes, lips pursed before spitting on his face.

Justin snickered and wiped off the spittle with his arm. "I'll consider that a parting gift. Any last words you want us to relay to Chris?"

"I'll see you in hell," Mario snarled.

"Understood."

Justin stood up, pistol still clenched in his grip and aimed it at Mario's stomach, pulling the trigger and walking away.

The entire team loaded back into the trucks, minus Sergio, who would fly the chopper back to Salt Lake City. The first domino had officially fallen in their mission to kill Chris. Justin only hoped things played out as smoothly in Chicago.

Chapter 5

Chris had called Thaddeus and requested an in-person meeting. He couldn't gauge the seriousness of Duane's accusations and wanted to read Thad for himself.

The two leaders agreed to meet at a downtown cafe in Cheyenne, Wyoming, a middle point between their residences in Idaho and Iowa.

"Mr. Hamilton," Chris greeted upon entering, two guards waiting outside. "Thank you so much for meeting me."

"Always an honor, Chris," Thad said, standing up to shake hands with the Keeper of Time. "What is this about?"

They chose a corner booth away from the other patrons chomping down their breakfast and coffee. "I wanted to check in with you. Matters have certainly escalated between us and the Road Runners. Plus it's been a few weeks since the Liberation officially formed their own leadership. Is there anything else you need help with? I'm here for you."

"It's been fun," Thaddeus said, chuckling. "A stressful sort of fun, but we're making strides. We're solid financially, but the issues we're running into are about structuring our organization. We obviously have exposure and experience with both the Revolution and Road Runners, and are trying to pull the best from both worlds. We've had debates about forming a

Council with checks and balances, and also if there should be a line of succession below me."

"Checks and balances will make your life a living hell," Chris said. "You deserve to rule as you please, don't you agree?"

Chris was drooling on the inside, Thaddeus giving him a grand opportunity to pick his mind regarding what exactly he wanted out of his role as the leader of the Liberation.

"Well, sure, that would be nice, but I don't have the luxury of invincibility like yourself. If I make a decision that my organization doesn't like, they can come and take me out."

Chris waved a hand as he grinned. "Thaddeus, you're the leader—*you* make the rules, *you* set your security in place. You can have a wall of guards around you at all times if you want. No one can lay a finger on you. This is a unique opportunity to build your organization from the ground up. Don't make the same mistakes as the Road Runners and try to be fair. One thing I've learned since becoming the Keeper of Time is that people will respect you for the sole reason of your position. People are brainwashed to respect titles, plain and simple. If you're the leader, you can refuse to listen to anyone else's ideas and structure things the way you want. Sometimes you just have to put your dick on the table and let people deal with it."

"How does being the Keeper of Time work? Is it something you can make in your lab and share? Have you ever considered splitting that power with others close to you?"

"Are you suggesting yourself?" Chris asked, cocking an eyebrow. *Are you trying to slip into the most powerful position in the world?* he wondered.

"I'm just curious how it works. No one seems to have a clear understanding."

"I'm afraid that's our most forbidden secret. It is only shared with the successor and no one else. Only past Keepers know about the process."

"I understand you keep some of your blood in Sonya for the sake of staying alive. If she lives, you can never die. But if your blood is so sacred, then why is it not enough on its own?"

"The Keeper of Time has always been a God-on-Earth, if you will. I don't know *how* it was discovered to maintain invincibility."

"And you know where Sonya is? I've been thinking of potential missions for the Liberation to focus on, and thought that helping with the Sonya matter could be a good way to get our feet wet."

"I know what year she is in, but not where," Chris lied, seeing the writing on the wall for Thaddeus. Any more questions about their biggest secrets, and he might have to slit the man's throat and walk out. "I keep tabs on her health for my own sake. She's doing just fine wherever she is."

"I get the feeling you're lying to me," Thaddeus said, his face stony as he glared across the table.

"And I feel you're prodding for information you don't need. What is it you really want with Sonya?"

Thaddeus tossed his hands up. "Look, Chris, we're just looking for ways to help. We're all grateful for the opportunity you've given to let us govern ourselves. Aside from figuring out those details, we're just looking for things to do."

"I see. I'm looking to build a new headquarters after this war is over. I'd also like help finding the other Warm Souls who live in other parts of the world. If we can find even one, then we'll have a leg up when Martin tries to make his move." Chris really wanted to see if he could send the Liberation out of the continent. If Thaddeus agreed to the offer, then Chris could dismiss Duane's absurd theory. But if he refused to leave, then what exactly might that prove?

"We'd love to work with you on the headquarters—we're looking to build one ourselves in a different location. I don't know about sending any Liberators across the ocean to hunt for Warm Souls. I'm not willing to lose any of our already small forces."

"But you just told me you're looking for something to do. This would be a huge step for both of us. Imagine a world with no Road Runners. The Liberation and Revolution could team up in peace and do as we please. That will never be possible unless I gain access to a Warm Soul."

"I understand, but I don't think we have the resources for that—we need to keep our advantage here on home turf. We'd love to help with this battle against Briar. Let us do so by protecting Sonya—just tell us the year and we'll track her down."

Chris closed his eyes and leaned his head back.

"I'm currently searching for a new number two," Chris said, dismissing Thad's request. "I've toyed with the idea of asking you. What are your thoughts on such a role?"

Chris knew this question would determine plenty. If Thaddeus really wanted to overthrow the Revolution, he'd have to reject the offer based on the terms laid out by Chris.

"How would that work?" Thad asked, Chris sitting forward with a grin, pulling all the strings in this mental chess battle. "I can't possibly be the number two in the Revolution *and* serve as the leader for the Liberation. I would be spread too thin."

"Of course not," Chris said. "I'm talking about a merger—"

"You guaranteed the Liberation an existence of peace to operate on our own."

Chris raised a gentle hand. "Simmer down, we're only having a discussion. I'm not suggesting the Liberation sacrifice their status and become Revolters. A merger would see our two organizations operate under the same umbrella. You would still be the Liberation, and as the number two in the Revolution, you could either continue to lead your particular subsidiary, or choose whoever you'd like to do so."

"So it's a demotion for me?"

Chris grinned. "That's a funny way of looking at it. I see it as a *promotion*. You'd be retaining your same role, with additional responsibilities, perhaps. But you'd have complete access to the entire Revolution's resources: our funds, soldiers, equipment, you name it. And I'd leave you free to do as you please, just ask Duane if you need any confirmation. I can't recall a time I ever rejected a proposal he wanted."

Thaddeus sunk back into the booth, fingers brushing over his chin as he entered deep thought. "I don't know. That's a big decision."

"I'm not asking you to commit to anything right now—hell, I don't even expect you to accept the offer. Just thought I'd throw it out there."

"Has anything like this been done before?"

"Not to my knowledge. Every time a group has branched off from the Revolution it's because they hated us and wanted to retaliate. But you branched off from the Road Runners. My enemy's enemy is my friend, and that's how I view the Liberation."

"And we feel the same, but I can't lie, Chris, I don't think I'm ready to give up my role. I'd love to keep working alongside the Revolution, but I want to see if we can make it on our own—with your guidance, but not necessarily your help, if that makes sense."

"How ambitious," Chris said. "But I understand and can't blame you. You're in that unique position of being able to operate without the constant threat of me wiping you off the planet, unlike the Road Runners. You still have my full support in whatever you need." Chris checked his watch. "I should probably get back—I've got lots to prepare for the coming days, which I suspect will be bloody."

Thaddeus stood, much taller than Chris as he towered over the Keeper. "I wish you the best. I'm sure it won't be easy, but you'll come out on top like always. When this all blows over, I'd love to get back together and talk about plans after the Road Runners."

"Now that's a conversation I very much look forward to," Chris said as he joined Thad in leaving the booth.

The two shook hands and left the café behind, parting ways as they returned to their private jets. Chris had all he needed from the brief meeting. When his jet rumbled to life and took off back to Idaho, one thought kept playing over in his mind.

I'm going to kill Thaddeus Hamilton.

Chapter 6

Nearly a century in the past, just as Chris touched back down in Idaho, Martin stood at Sonya's door, adrenaline bursting through his veins as his life flashed before his eyes. He knocked a second time, harder, to ensure it was heard. Eyes had been on all doors that exited the complex for the past thirty-six hours, and no one had reported Sonya leaving the building. She was in there, though—no doubt about it.

He knocked a third time, sternly, to let her know he wasn't leaving. His hands remained in the air despite his brain urging him to grab a weapon.

Don't tell me she just vanishes into the past as soon as someone knocks, Martin thought. They had people spread throughout time for this measure, but it could take a while for that communication to reach Martin, depending on what year she traveled to. Regardless, he kept faith that she was hiding in the corner, waiting for him to leave.

Just as he was about to knock again, a shadow appeared from under the other side of the door, followed by Sonya's voice which sent chills down Martin's back. "Who's there?"

His throat clenched shut for a moment, suffocated by nerves. He had to mentally claw his mouth open to speak. "Sonya? It's me . . . Martin." The words came out shaky and soft, and he needed to snap out of it if he had plans of strong-arming Sonya.

He stared at the door for an entire minute, wondering if she had an exit plan of her own. If he knew her as well as he thought, then she certainly had a plan for any potential action that might arise in her new life on the run.

Instead of running, however, the apartment door swung open, Sonya appearing with a shotgun aimed at Martin, a bulletproof vest strapped over her chest. "What are you doing here, Martin?" she asked, eyes dancing around the empty hallway in search of any other potential threats.

Martin remained with his hands in the air and now felt stuck that way with a gun in his face. He'd never seen so much fear and rage swimming behind Sonya's eyes. Part of him wanted to run, but he also wanted to stay and throw his arms around her, hugging her until she suggested they run away together. He took a sharp gulp of the spit that had formed in his mouth before speaking.

"I just want to talk. I mean no harm."

"Then why are you dressed like this? Why do you have a gun?"

"To protect myself," Martin said, confidence slowly returning. "If you recall, you shot me two times."

"Let it go, Martin. I didn't know who to trust then—and I still don't."

"I'm not saying you have to trust to me, but I'm not going to hurt you—you should know that by now."

Sonya kept looking down the hallway, a black baseball cap low on her brow to shield her eyes. "You can come in, but I am *not* moving this gun away from you." She took two steps back to allow him to enter.

Martin hesitated, his legs wobbly as he took uncertain steps to enter the apartment. From the doorway he caught a glimpse of a well-kept living room: colorful throw rugs, art on the walls, and a wide sofa facing the radio. It was a flash of nostalgia from the time Martin lived with Sonya in her 1996 home.

"Sit at the kitchen table," she snapped, quickly pointing the shotgun toward the kitchen and moving it back to the commander.

Martin did as instructed, moving through the living room and to the kitchen where a pot of coffee brewed on the stove-top, its aroma filling the room. He was pleased to find the layout was the same as his, providing the comfort of familiarity.

"Take your gun out and put it on the table across from you. If I even *think* you're going to turn it on me, I'm pulling the trigger."

The immediate threat on his life forced a tremble back into Martin's arms as he debated the best position to angle his body and arms as to not startle Sonya. He decided to face sideways where she could watch him grab his pistol while not having it point in her direction, keeping his right hand in the air as he spoke through his process to hopefully relax her mind. "I'm reaching for my gun and will keep it aimed to the floor." He grabbed it, fighting to keep his hand still and wondering if she noticed his worry. "I'm moving it to the table and pushing it across to the other side." He did so and took a step back, relieved to have literally dodged a bullet.

"Stay there and let me sit down across from you," Sonya said, swiftly moving across the living room and around the kitchen table, sitting behind Martin's pistol and promptly planting her elbows over it. "You can sit now."

Martin slowly lowered himself into the chair, tension thick in the air and pounding on his head.

"What do you want from me, *Commander*?" she scoffed, clearly pissed that Martin was sitting in her apartment.

He believed nothing he said would be well-received, even if he offered to say "nevermind" and leave. So he decided to see where a normal conversation would lead them, keeping in mind that he now had to convince her to come with him. Killing her was off the table for the time being.

"How have you been?"

The question clearly caught her off guard, her eyes twitching toward the door as if she expected someone to barge in for an ambush. She remained silent for an awkward amount of time.

"I've had better days—a better life."

"You've really turned this place into a home," Martin said, looking around. "I think about you often . . . not just our romance, but just in general, and hope that you're okay."

Sonya rolled her eyes.

"Don't tell me you haven't thought back on our time together," Martin said, forcing a coy grin.

"Martin, I don't know how many times I need to tell you, what we had was nothing of significance. I ran through that same routine with plenty of other recruits before you. I was just doing my job—you're the one who can't let that go."

"Was it your job to get that medicine for my mom? Or to come cry at the hospital after my accident?"

"Just because you were a mission doesn't mean *I* have no soul. I lived with your mother—*that* was part of the job. I grew fond of her and didn't want to hear of her pain if there was something I could do to help."

"How kind of you. Do you ever miss your old life? You had it made when you were a Road Runner, back when you had a truce with Chris to leave you alone. I don't understand your

37

change of heart. You used to threaten him you'd kill yourself if he tried to interfere with your life."

"Only until *you* tried to kill me. I may be on the run from both Chris and the Road Runners, but it was the Road Runners who made me run in the first place."

"Why did you pick the Great Depression to hide?" Martin asked. "Seems like you could have gone anywhere."

"It's easy to hide here—people are so down on themselves that they don't pay attention to the world around them. Enough with the interrogation. The real question is, how did you find me?"

"I made a vow to bring an end to this war, and that's what I plan to do. You know we have the best talent around; finding you was by no means an impossible task."

Sonya's grip tightened on the shotgun, and Martin thought for sure she was done with this conversation—and his life. But she never pulled the trigger, instead shaking her head as a lone tear rolled down her face.

"What's wrong?" Martin asked, wanting to reach out and grab her hand for comfort, but was terrified of making any sudden movements.

Sonya shrugged, leaning back, keeping that tight grip on the shotgun. "It's like I've reached a dead end. I've worked so hard to scout locations and find somewhere to live in peace. But here you are. All I've wanted since I ran was to be left alone, but I have to call and check in with Chris every week to let him know I'm still alive and breathing. Like I'm his fucking life support. That call is planned for later tonight, by the way—maybe you want to hang around and say hello so you can both have a good laugh about me."

"Sonya, that's just not true, and you know it."

"Then why are you here?!" she snapped, freeing a hand and slamming a fist on the table. "Both of you have been harassing me and I'm so sick of it. I'm trapped in this apartment all day every day, can't even go out for a walk in the park because I have to constantly look over my shoulder—even when I know I should be safe, which I'm clearly *not* if you found me so easily. I don't doubt Chris has eyes on me too. Time travel has ruined my life. The Road Runners once brought me joy and purpose after my dad *completely* fucked my life, but ever since Strike decided my life was worth the cost of killing Chris, I've had a hard time finding the will to live."

"That's a funny thing to say, considering how far you've made it surviving."

"Surviving and living are two different things, you should know that. All those years you wasted after Izzy died and your divorce, drinking and drugs every night . . . that's not living."

"Fair, but it's really not surviving, either. You could say I was trying to kill myself with all of that. I only went to work so I didn't have to live on the street. I'd go right back home, no friends, no family aside from my mom, and trap myself in my apartment." Martin looked around with a grin. "I guess we're not that different after all."

Sonya nodded, removing her hat and dropping it on the table, running a hand through her hair. "I suppose we're not. I've definitely had suicidal thoughts since this all started, but those have dated back to childhood. Watching my mother get murdered then tossed away like a piece of trash screwed me up from the start. I've had time to reflect on my life—really all there is to do when you're trapped inside—and that's definitely what formed all of my trust issues with the universe. It's funny, even when I lived in the future in Chris's penthouse suite, I still

39

had these dark thoughts creep in. The unlimited shopping sprees, fancy dinners, dates with the most handsome men Chris knew. It was all designed to give me a sort of superficial pleasure. But people don't understand that the simple ability to do as you please, live wherever you want with whoever you want—that's the real wealth."

Martin nodded, pleased to have Sonya pouring out her heart. He hoped to flip that vulnerability around and use it for good. "Look, Sonya, I want to end this war. I want Chris dead and dismembered. And I want to achieve all of that without harming you. I didn't come here to kill you—I came to reach out a hand and bring you back to the Road Runners. I can protect you, hide you, you name it. You can live in my house—*our* house. It's fully guarded and no one gets inside unless I say so. We can work on this together and move beyond the ugly ending that you previously had."

Sonya shook her head. "It's too dangerous. I heard about the ultimatum that Chris gave the Road Runners, making them choose between you and Strike. Pure chaos. If I returned, I know there would be plenty of Road Runners wanting to hunt me down."

"No one will know. Just myself and the security team."

"And what if someone on the security team wants me dead? Or the Council? I know how this works, Martin. You're the commander—lots of people already know where you are and *why* you're here right now. That alone is already too many people. And how many people are in this building right now? Probably hiding near all the exits, right?"

Martin fell silent, letting his gaze fall to the table.

"You forget I spent a very long time with the Road Runners and had friends in high places. I know how it all works. The commander doesn't just get to hop on the jet and fly across the country because he feels like it. And I'm sure it's even more strict since Strike was killed. How many people are here, Martin? Don't lie. Twenty? Thirty?"

Martin licked his lips, now wishing he was the one who could bolt out of the room. Out of this life. "Twenty-four of us have been living here for the past two weeks."

Sonya grinned, shaking her head. "Unbelievable. You sick bastard. If you actually loved me, like you claim, then you'd know to leave me alone. You'd let me live my life. I'm going back with you today, aren't I? I don't have a say in the matter."

"I'm not forcing you to do anything," Martin said in the flattest voice he could muster. He felt like an amateur poker player who got caught trying to bluff a veteran. His hand was in the cookie jar and he had nowhere to turn.

"Right. It's not *you* who will force me, but one of your people waiting outside. Let me guess, you planted others at this location all throughout time, didn't you? That's what a good, well-planned mission would look like."

Martin pursed his lips, several beads of sweat forming on his head, unable to wipe them away in case Sonya decided his movement warranted a death penalty.

"You're right," he said. "I don't know what you want me to say."

"Well, you're the commander, so you can stand up and leave, and order everyone else to go with you. Then never come back here."

"I wish it was that simple. This mission was authorized by the Council—my team has strict orders to carry out this mission regardless of what happens to me."

New tears welled in Sonya's eyes, streaming quicker down

41

her face. "You truly surprise me—always have. I never thought I'd see the day where you turned into the enemy, but here you are, sitting right at my fucking table."

"Sonya—"

"Shut your mouth, Martin. You can't sweet talk your way out of this now. You've dug your grave, and now you must live with it."

Martin gulped, convinced the slug would knock his lights out in just a few moments. Ironically, the only person he had any desire to say goodbye to sat right across the table.

"I'm leaving this apartment when *I* say it's time," Sonya snarled. "Now tell me, what is the plan? We all get on the jet and sing 'Kumbaya' while we fly to Denver? I know everything is planned to the final detail. Humor me."

Martin's throat had tensed shut again, and he had to fight to simply get the words out. "They're going to kill you."

Sonya snorted. "Shocker. Are you just now realizing that you're the pawn in this game they're playing? Or have you thought you were calling the shots all along? Now I have to wonder if I was also the pawn, sent to recruit the man who would one day be used to capture me. The circle of life, I suppose. We just use each other until death, then move on to the next valuable person."

Martin felt tears of his own forming, blinking rapidly to not let them appear. The tension in the apartment brought the stillness of impending death, the sensation crawling over his skin like spiders. He tried to piece together all the actions and decisions that led to this exact moment, but his mind was too scattered to make any true sense of it. The Council had essentially forced this mission, but not necessarily him as the one to do it. Did they know he would volunteer, knowing he couldn't resist the opportunity to see Sonya in the flesh for what would be the final time? Did they care if he was killed on this mission? They had been so strict with the rules about guards never leaving Martin's side, until this most dangerous portion of the mission.

The walls closed in around Martin, his heart rate and breathing increasing by the second. "Sonya, we can run together. I can buy us time to get out of here."

She shook her head vigorously side to side. "I don't think so—this is the finish line. I can't even be mad at you. We were both pawns in this war, used with *and* against each other. The Road Runners are brilliant, I'll give them that much. Don't you see, this only ends one way—with me dead. You admitted you can't even control the people they sent with you. They picked someone just smart enough to be called a commander, but dumb enough to not realize he was being played. Combine that with your emotions for me, and it was the perfect storm. Once I successfully recruited you, that was checkmate as far as the Road Runners were concerned—just a matter of figuring out the logistics to make it all work and appear like a natural occurrence. Bravo, Road Runners, you win!" she screamed, followed by a psychotic laughter that echoed her father.

"Sonya, please. At least let me try to talk my way out of this with everyone outside."

"I already told you, I'm leaving when *I* decide it's time. I don't need your help running. Did your people even think of the roof? I have exits all over this place, on purpose. You still haven't told me the rest of the plan, and I need to know before I leave here."

Martin nodded, conceding this mission, conceding his life. If he made it back to Denver, he had no idea how he'd face the

Council or the membership again. Sonya had planted too much doubt about his actual role in the organization. Did the other commanders secretly agree to a pact to get rid of Chris, despite their clear opposition on all their group phone calls? They were the ones who endorsed Martin and ensured him a victory. It had grown clear that the organization as a whole had no problem eliminating one or two members if it guaranteed peace.

"The plan . . ." Martin said, convinced these would be the final words spoken of his storied life. "The plan is to kill you, then kill Chris before he has time to realize you're gone."

"Does that mean there are people already waiting for the word of my death?"

Martin shook his head. "Not exactly. I'm supposed to go kill him. I've been in contact with an old friend from Europe, Steffan Privvy. He's going to freeze time for us and allow me to face Chris one-on-one."

Sonya nodded. "It sounds so simple when you put it like that, but we all know how many factors are out of your control. My life is one. *Your* life is another. Things have to fall into place so perfectly, and here you are, knocking on the door of your destiny to be the greatest commander in the history of an organization you know nothing about. The world is a beautiful, romantic place, isn't it? Do you ever think about fate, Martin? Have you ever taken the time to look at the map of your life and see how everything fell perfectly into place to land you where you are today?"

"Sure, sometimes."

"I do it all the time. Every single day. When I wake up in this shitty apartment, in this shitty year, I wonder, what on Earth brought me here? After I graduated high school I could've gone anywhere. Could've moved to Australia and started a new life. But I was so sheltered, afraid to take such a wild gamble. And I hated my dad, so when the opportunity arose to join the organization that hates him as much as me, I dove into their open arms. That was my first mistake. But here's what I've realized: they already knew. The Road Runners have a copy of your map, you see. They study lives, see what paths lie ahead for everyone they recruit. They're patient—always playing the long game. They have to since they can't match the resources Chris has.

"Once I was inside the Road Runner bubble, my pathway was already set for me without realizing it. I had the impression that I was directing my own life, but they put tracking chips into us, for God's sake. I wasn't in control of anything. They always know to set up their pawns for the best position possible to further their agenda. Whoever is calling the shots knew this moment would come, but they can't account for what will happen in the heat of the moment. What happens if I shoot you? Then there is no one to encounter Chris with time frozen—back to square one. Either way, I don't make it out of this building alive."

"Sonya, I can help. Just let me. Please."

"I've recently spent my time looking ahead instead of back, trying to see what lies ahead on my map of life. I don't see a moment where my life can return to normal. I will always be on the run, always worried about someone trying to shoot me. My life has been reduced to that of a caged animal, but I have no one to blame but myself. Mental awareness will keep you out of unwanted situations, but too many factors play with our emotions to let us see straight."

Tears flooded from her eyes, the lower half of her face glistening from the moisture. She wiped her nose and lowered the shotgun, not quite letting it go.

Martin still refused to make a movement, not understanding what was happening. "Sonya?"

Her head had dropped toward the floor, tears splashing onto her lap. It was a silent cry, no heaving, not even a tremble in her shoulders. She raised her head, watery eyes falling on Martin. "I've seen the hand I've been dealt, and I've been left no choice. I hope you can forgive me, Martin, but you and I both need to do the right thing. Go take care of business. I love you."

Sonya flipped the shotgun back up, inserting the muzzle into her mouth.

"NOOOOOO!" Martin jumped from his chair, lunging across the table, the moment coming to a momentary standstill just before Sonya pulled the trigger, her blood and brains decorating the refrigerator and kitchen walls behind her. The shotgun slid in slow motion from her hands, clattering on the floor.

Martin landed on the table, causing it to collapse under his weight, as he crashed to the floor with a heavy thud, his flailing hands brushing Sonya's dead legs on the way down. He rolled to the side, bumped into the trash can, and hurried to his knees to vomit inside of it.

After hurling his breakfast for a minute, Martin brought himself up on his trembling legs, the room spinning around him as he fought the urge to faint. His radio crackled something inaudible, surely someone on the team having heard the gunshot and demanding an explanation.

He stared across the kitchen to Sonya, her body still seated in the chair, head cocked all the way back as blood oozed from her mouth, more of it pooling beneath the hole on the back of her head. His entire body shook, reminding him of the way the world shook after drinking the Juice and bracing to travel through time.

Rapid, panicked knocking came from the front door, but Martin could only manage a step before he collapsed to the floor, crying.

Chapter 7

Martin didn't follow the protocol of paging the team if he managed to kill Sonya. Then again, he didn't kill Sonya.

"Commander Briar!" Arielle's voice cried from the other side of the door. She had remained hidden on the third floor, keeping the closest eye on Sonya's apartment door, ready to pounce if she bolted out. "Commander, is everything okay?!"

Her voice, despite being muffled through the wooden door, sounded desperate and worried. Martin crawled toward the living room couch, leaning back against it as he entered a state of shock. Sonya's sacrifice had not been on the list of possibilities, leaving Martin flustered with regard of what to do.

Go take care of business, he thought, reminiscing on her finals words. It was no accident. She had made a calculated decision to pull that trigger and set in motion the hunt for Chris. As much as he needed to hurry to ensure everything fell into place with their plans, Martin needed the moment to process what he had just witnessed.

"Commander, I'm breaking down this door!" Arielle cried.

The banging from outside fell momentarily silent, followed by a sharp *bang!* that saw the door swing open, Arielle standing on one leg while the other remained elevated from kicking.

Martin rolled his head to look at her, watching her eyes bounce from him to Sonya, then to the shotgun that lay on the floor at her feet.

"Commander?" Arielle asked, inching into the apartment with the caution of a burglar.

Martin felt the puffiness in his eyes, knowing they were surely red from the ten minutes he had just spent crying. "She shot herself," he said, the words stiff out of his lips. "I didn't even see it coming—I thought she was going to shoot *me*." His lips quivered as he fought off another wave of tears, mind still catching up to the fact that his life had been spared. Martin had survived plenty of trauma throughout his life, but this encounter had been the most intense thanks to its rapid progression. Even the loss of Izzy had been a gradual process of acceptance as the days passed, creating a different kind of shock.

Arielle wasted no time in grabbing her radio and speaking into it. "Everyone stand down, stay in your positions. Lieutenant Commander, please come to Sonya's apartment, it is now safe."

Martin flailed for the couch to help him stand, eventually doing so with the struggle of a toddler just learning to pull themselves up. Once on his feet, Martin forced his legs to walk away from the scene in the kitchen and meet Arielle in the doorway. "Come inside and close the door—we can't afford to have a neighbor wander this way."

He knew this wasn't necessarily a worry considering the year—suicides were quite commonplace during the Depression, plenty of reports eventually leaking that neighbors, and even family members, would hear gunshots from around the way, knowing what had happened but not bothering to confirm—but

49

they still couldn't afford the gamble of leaving the door wide open.

Arielle obliged, closing the door and pressing her back against it now that the latch didn't work thanks to her well-placed kick. "Commander, I know this a lot for you right now, but once the lieutenant gets here, we need to move fast. Remember, we projected six to eight hours until Chris realizes he's mortal again. At that point, we have no idea what exactly he will do."

"I know. We can start." Martin's chest felt drained, void of all emotion. His brain understood exactly what needed to happen next, even insisted on it, but his heart wasn't in it. Not yet. Gone was the anger that had driven him to this point, a hate sparked by the death of his mother, then elevated by learning that Sonya had killed Gerald outside of Chris's Idaho home. All that remained, for the moment, were the raw emotions of losing a loved one. A future together was no longer an option, leaving Martin truly alone.

A knock came from the door and Arielle stepped aside to pull it open and let Alina enter. Her jaw dropped at the horrific scene. Martin gave the abbreviated story of what had happened, able to make it through this second telling with a bit more composure.

"It's time, Commander," Alina said. "Regardless of how this played out, this is what we came for. Chris Speidel is now a mortal human being, and we have to act before he tries to change that fact."

Martin nodded. "Inform the appropriate teams. We can begin phase one, just make sure no one is around to relay the events to Chris."

"Arielle, can you please hop into the future and make that

call?"

"Yes, ma'am," Arielle replied, promptly leaving the apartment to head outside where she'd jump forward in time to place a phone call to the team waiting to tail Chris.

Once they were alone, Alina moved toward Martin and placed an arm over his shoulder. "We all know this was going to be hard for you, Commander. But look at where we are now. This war will be done by tonight and we can start our road to recovery and peace."

"I don't feel so hopeful," Martin said, giving into Alina's embrace as his legs still weren't quite ready to support the rest of him. Sonya had done a number on his mind by planting a seed of doubt regarding his role with the Road Runners. While it all seemed a stretch, nothing in her theory could be deemed as impossible. Could the Council have orchestrated this whole ordeal? Or another commander from a different continent? Possible, but not likely. As commander, Martin had access to too much information, not to mention the teams that worked under him all around North America. If this had been the grand scheme, then everyone would have been carefully chosen to work directly with Martin—yet he was the one who picked Alina Herrera to replace Gerald. And had picked Gerald in the first place. For now, he needed to focus and would worry about piecing together this puzzle later.

"The hope is there, and it's our little secret. I made the decision that we will not be relaying any information back to the Council as originally planned. Only those who have roles in critical missions will be informed when it is their time to act. The less people who know what is happening, the better off we'll be."

Martin scrunched his face, stepping out of Alina's embrace

to face her straight on. "I don't understand."

"Look, we know Chris has always been able to hack into our network and systems. And after the debacle with Councilwoman Murray, I've concluded we can't take any chances at this point. We can't come this far to let a potential slip-up beyond our control derail this entire mission. If any mistakes are made, they'd better be from you or me."

Alina spoke with such conviction that Martin had no choice but to trust her. It also eased his mind about her being planted in his life. If she wanted to keep the Council out of the loop—something that would shortly send them and the entire Road Runner membership into a frenzy—then she was, without a doubt, solely focused on killing Chris. In this moment, Martin witnessed the height of Alina's character, and knew she would one day serve as a fine commander.

"How much time does that buy us before the Council comes looking?"

"The Council won't find us—I've already given strict instruction to our team to not answer any calls from the Council, or to reach out to anyone besides me. You and I need to work on this eight-hour deadline and get the job done."

Martin grinned for the first time since arriving to this apartment, but remained void of actual emotion. "I'm glad to have you here. I know Gerald would have done great in this role, but I feel such a different kind of calm with you around."

"I appreciate that, Commander. Gerald was a hero and legend within our organization, especially in my line of work. I had the pleasure of doing a couple missions with him. Now, I want you to gather yourself. We don't have to step out of this room until you feel more together, but that needs to happen soon. I'll wait in the hallway and will have someone call a team to clean up this apartment. Do you have any preference what we should do with Sonya's body?"

Martin hadn't considered the question before, not realizing the decision would ultimately be left to him as the commander. Surely it had been planned to some degree by his team and they wanted to leave the thought out of his mind.

"Arrange to have her buried next to my daughter. Larkwood Cemetery. Take her back to 2020 and bury her there."

"As you wish, Commander. Any other requests for her burial?"

"That will be all, thank you."

Alina nodded and left the apartment, Martin looking to Sonya for the final time, his heart tearing apart at the seams.

"I love you," he said. "You were a star in my night, my only beacon of hope. I don't know if we would have ever gotten the timing right, but I'll always remember our time together. It didn't have to end this way, and I'll spend the rest of my days trying to figure out why you felt it did. I'll think about your hugs, your lips, your scent. The way you'd giggle sometimes in your sleep. All I wanted was the chance to love you and help you heal from the wounds of your past. I suppose all I can do now is honor your life by completing this mission. Thank you for trying to save my mom—that's all I needed to know about your true character. I'll never forget you."

Martin blew a kiss across the room before he turned and left, wiping the tears away to move to the next phase of this ultimate mission.

Chapter 8

Chris didn't know he was mortal, and he still wouldn't for a few more hours. He was too occupied to notice the grumbling in his stomach, or even the yawns that escaped his mouth for the first time in decades.

Instead, he was focused on abolishing the Liberation, just as he had done to all the other pathetic organizations that had tried to rise up in the past—except for the Road Runners, of course. He had called Duane, seeking advice from his longtime confidant, but he didn't answer on three different attempts, adding an extra layer of frustration for the Keeper of Time.

Sure, he could barge into Thad's home and shoot him, but alone he wouldn't be able to withstand the guaranteed retaliation of doing such a thing. Even with his assumed invincibility, he had no chance of outrunning a mob of pissed off time travelers.

He had a small team now, all made up of his brainwashed soldiers, and they would have to suffice through the remainder of this war. He also had a team at Wealth of Time, but they weren't equipped to fight, focusing more on recruitment efforts around the continent. Chris had called for a temporary pause in recruiting, not wanting to further expand their operation until he had help running the organization.

After plenty of contemplation, Chris decided that he'd be the one to remove Thaddeus Hamilton from the world. "We've been pushed around enough these last few weeks," Chris said to his houseful of soldiers, ready to do as he commanded. "Our task is a simple one. We'll let ourselves into his house, maybe even position it as a peaceful meeting—I'll need to chat with him first and get a feel for the mood. I don't believe he knows that I know his absurd goals for trying to overthrow me as the Keeper of Time. Your task will be to eliminate anyone else in the house, and capture Thaddeus—leave him for me."

These words echoed on the early morning flight to central Iowa, the soldiers getting amped up for the busy day ahead. Chris had called to find Thaddeus was indeed in high spirits, welcoming the unexpected visit from Chris and his soldiers on the grounds of discussing possible options for the capture of Martin Briar.

It didn't take much to excite the eager Liberation, and Chris played to their leader's ambitious emotions. There was no plan for getting Martin, and if there was, it certainly wouldn't be shared with Thaddy at this point in time.

"An easy blindside mission, boys," Chris said when they had arrived and departed the jet. An organization as small and young as the Liberation would have no way of surviving the assassination of its leader so early in their existence. They likely had no plans in place for such an event, and would scramble for a few weeks before eventually fizzling into the void of failed organizations.

All guns were loaded and ready—Chris just needing to give the signal once they arrived to Thad's home in Ames, Iowa. He had moved from his prior San Francisco residence where Chris had first encountered him at the beginning of their relationship.

The Liberation had originally formed in Iowa, a majority of its members having lived in the state. It became an unofficial headquarters despite not having a building to call home.

Thaddeus hosted many events each month from his house, primarily ones that required their small leadership team to make plans for the future. Thad took the liberty of inviting a handful of these leaders for the occasion of Chris's visit.

Chris drooled when Thad mentioned this on the phone, knowing the bloodbath that awaited. By the time they arrived to Thad's house in two separate vans, Chris and his team had a perfect understanding of how the morning was supposed to play out. The beauty of being the Keeper of Time was that no one questioned when Chris arrived to a destination with his dozen of guards surrounding him, guns in hand.

"What a beautiful house, don't you think?" Chris asked his team as they unloaded from the vans and started up the flagstone pathway that split the front yard into two halves. Yellow and orange leaves sprinkled the lawn from the massive oak tree that shaded the garage to their right.

Chris saw through the front window a group of four men laughing in the living room, standing around with drinks in hand. He rang the doorbell and took a step back. *These boys like to party early.*

Thaddeus opened the door, a tipsy grin plastered across his face. "Chris Speidel! You should have just come home with me after our meeting in Wyoming—would have saved the extra trip."

"No worries at all," Chris said as he led his team into the house. "I had business to tend to back in Idaho—I don't mind the time on the jet, gives me a moment to unplug from the chaos."

Thaddeus chuckled as he held the door open for all twelve soldiers. "Well, I hope we can help take some of the workload off your shoulders. We've already been talking things over about how to get Briar."

"Oh really? I can't wait to hear. Where should I have the team mingle? I'm sorry for traveling so heavy, but times are dangerous right now."

"No problem at all," Thaddeus said, turning to the men crowded into the foyer and living room. "Gentlemen, I have plenty of space in the backyard or basement. Make yourselves at home and let me know if you need anything."

The lead soldier nodded and made his way down the only visible hallway, all others following him.

"Thank you," Chris said.

"Can I get you anything? Beer? Water?"

"I'm okay, thank you. I run on a tight schedule, as you might imagine, so I'd love to jump into business if that works for you fine gentlemen."

"Absolutely. Let me introduce you to the gang." Thaddeus pivoted and strolled to the three other men who had waited in the opposite corner of the living room, sofas and lounge chairs set up around the perimeter, a coffee table moved in front of the fireplace to open the space up. "We've broken our organization into four different regions to start. I lead what we call Liberation Midwest. And here we have Joe Hicks, leader of our West Coast and Rocky Mountain branch."

A tall man stepped forward, his face long and droopy, black hair matted down in a way that reminded Chris of Frankenstein's monster. "Pleasure to meet you," he said in a deep voice that greatly complemented his appearance.

"And Morgan Kuzma, leader of our Northeast branch,"

Thaddeus said, moving to the next man, a more sophisticated appearance with his glasses and sweater vest, a perfectly-trimmed goatee framing his welcoming grin. Chris shook hands with him and offered a smile. "And last, but not least, Donny Spencer, leader of our Southern region."

Donny nodded to Chris but didn't speak, keeping a tight-lipped grin before forcing his beer back to his mouth.

"Quite the team you've assembled here. How many members are you at now?" Chris asked.

"We're approaching four thousand scattered across the country. We have even shifted our focus beyond the U.S. borders—hoping to find a new recruit who gels with all of us and make them the leader of our international efforts. Right now we are solely focused on recruiting new members from the Road Runners. There's still plenty of them out there who are sick of the status quo and want a new opportunity."

"Impressive, and you plan on using these recruits to help track down Briar?"

"That's the plan. Most of these recruits are eager to completely break away from the Road Runners and declare their allegiance to the Liberation. But we have left some that we call 'floaters' to sort of go back and forth. They attend Road Runner meetings, stay in the know, and relay that information to us. We could still do that ourselves, but don't feel like it."

The Liberators all stared at each other and broke into cocky laughter. Chris joined them, disappointed that he'd have to kill such a fun group of guys, who he'd surely enjoy working alongside if they didn't have cruel intentions in their hearts.

"Well, I'll admit, I like what I'm hearing so far," Chris said, now curious to hear what sort of information they might have obtained. "Have you made a plan, or done any research into capturing Briar? I had to jump through all sorts of hoops and bribes to snatch Strike when I did. It was a precise window of opportunity that could have been squandered if I hadn't been ready. I know how hard this is."

"It's much easier for us still being members of the Road Runners. We can check the news, even request meetings with prominent leaders around the continent. We've checked out the Denver office and Briar's house—those places are truly impenetrable right now. Our best bet is to find him out of town and try to catch him off guard."

"But there's a big problem right now," Joe said.

Thaddeus nodded. "Yes. It doesn't appear—at least to us—that anyone knows where Briar is at the moment."

Chris had been too occupied to have checked on his old friend in recent weeks, and this news was a surprise, especially coming directly from the Road Runners. "I'm sure he's in the trenches, planning his next attack on me."

"What can we do today to get started?" Thaddeus asked, the room falling silent as the mood had shifted all the way to serious.

Chris let his eyes wander toward the hallway where he saw his lead soldier waiting at the end. He grinned before turning his attention back to the Liberators gathered in the living room, ready for the fireworks to begin any moment.

"I don't know," Chris said. "We can certainly dig into the research you've already completed. I don't have any on my end yet for Briar specifically, but I suppose a good amount of it translates from Strike. Another positive is that it's back on my home turf of Colorado." The men looked at him, puzzled. Everyone associated Chris with his Alaskan mansion and never thought twice about his origins. "I'm from Colorado

Springs—a decent drive from Denver, but I'm plenty familiar with the area."

Chris saw three soldiers out of the corner of his eyes, lurching in the hallway. "By the way, did I mention what a beautiful home you have, Thaddy? The *feng shui* is exquisite."

He grinned and took two steps back, having given his code phrase of *feng shui*. The three soldiers barreled down the hallway as Thaddeus thanked Chris for the compliment, oblivious.

They reached the living room and immediately opened fire on the other three Liberators, glasses crashing to the ground in beautiful symphony, shortly followed by the heavy thumps of dead bodies hitting the hardwood floor.

"Oops," Chris said, offering a polite giggle.

Thaddeus dropped his glass without second thought, his hands held high in the air. "Chris? What is this?" he asked, his voice coming out both shocked and mixed with a wary confidence.

"Don't play dumb with me," Chris snarled. "I know what you're up to and I won't stand by and let it happen."

Thaddeus gulped, shaking his head in slow motion. "I don't know what's going on, but this is treason, Chris. Do you understand what you've done? We have to retaliate—you just killed our entire leadership."

"Well, not yet," Chris said with a crooked smile.

Thaddeus dropped his arms, fear vanishing from his eyes as he realized death was imminent. "You played me. Pulled me along on this big joke, huh?"

"Quite the contrary, Mr. Hamilton. I had no issue letting you operate as an individual organization, but our meeting in Wyoming left a sour taste in my mouth. I didn't appreciate all of the questions regarding my Keeper abilities. I'm afraid I can't let anyone live who even suggests threatening that status. I already have my hands full and can't fight two battles at the same time."

"Whoa, whoa, whoa!" Thaddeus cried, desperation replacing his short-lived confidence. "Don't kill me, Chris. I don't know what conclusions you're jumping to, but I think you have it all wrong."

"I'm sure you say that now because it's convenient. Do you even know how many times I've been crossed since becoming the Keeper?"

Thaddeus didn't respond.

"More than I can even keep track of," Chris said. "I've killed people in my past and don't even remember their names, all because they thought it would be fun to dance with the Revolution. Now, I'll admit you pose no direct threat to the Revolution, but if the Keeper status is what you want, I won't stand for that."

"Chris, you can't go on forever. You need help," Thaddeus said in his last ditch effort to spare his life. "And whether or not it's me, someone will replace you eventually. We can work out a transition, something that allows you to retain power and respect across the world."

Chris nodded for his soldiers to grab Thaddeus and they promptly did so, one each grabbing an arm, the other keeping a distance with his rifle aimed at his head.

"How generous of you, Thaddy, but I'll be fine on my own—just like I've been my entire life. I am curious, was this your play all along? Was it ever about showing up the Road Runners, or was this the moment you longed for?"

"I've never thought of taking anything from you, Chris. I wish you'd recognize that. You're making a mistake."

Chris pulled out his pistol, admired it, and tucked it back into waistband. He rummaged through his pockets until whipping out a switchblade, promptly ejecting the knife and taking a slow step toward Thaddeus who started squirming in the guards' grips. "I don't make mistakes," Chris said, forcing the blade through Thad's throat, holding it in place as the Liberation's leader gurgled on his own blood, then pulling it out and licking both sides of the blade clean before returning it to his pocket.

Chris stepped back and watched as Thad's legs gave out, blood squirting from his throat like a fountain, decorating the living room. Some even landed on Chris's face, but he didn't notice, too busy beaming into Thad's eyes as life slipped away and raw fear emerged from his pores like a seductive gas.

Chris opened his nostrils and took a deep inhale, feeding his soul, lusting for the opportunity to have a similar moment with Martin Briar.

Chapter 9

Chris ordered the team three rounds of drinks for their flight back to Idaho. Flights with his soldiers were typically silent, but Chris encouraged them to celebrate this special occasion by eating, drinking, playing cards, and even smoking cigars. It was a small victory they all needed to boost their morale after the tumult of the past month.

He really needed to return his focus to Briar and the Road Runners. Thaddeus had proven that Chris could be too easily distracted with other threats, and let his guard down for that hour in his Iowa home. Anything could have happened during that hour, and Chris needed to keep that in mind.

They all shared a laugh before landing in Idaho, mocking Thaddeus for thinking he could get away with such ambition.

"Would someone on their last leg as Keeper be able to sniff out that bullshit and put a swift end to it?!" Chris asked his raucous jet of soldiers.

"NO!" they all barked in response.

"Does the Keeper of Time ever quit?!"

"NO!"

"Does the Keeper of Time bow down to his enemies?!"

"NO!"

"Will the Keeper of Time ever die?!"

"HELL NO!"

They broke into chaotic cheering, some of the large men even jumping around, the jet feeling like it had caught a bout of mild turbulence. Chris fell back into his lounge chair, laughing to the ceiling.

As was always the case, celebrations only lasted so long for the Revolution. Once they landed and hit the road for their hour drive to Three Creek, Chris had already shifted his focus to the next task at hand. It was Monday, and that meant an incoming phone call from Sonya was scheduled for exactly 3:45 P.M.

He had twenty minutes to spare once they arrived to the house, and Chris used the time on his laptop, browsing the live feed of the Road Runners' news network. There were no stories of significance—mostly uplifting crap that he had no interest hearing about.

Sonya had been on her own for over a month now, and had always called at the exact day and time they had agreed on. Chris, a man of his word, had indeed refused to look into Sonya's whereabouts, trusting their agreement of her checking in once a week to ensure she was breathing and well.

He closed the Road Runners' feed at 3:44 and leaned back in his office chair, arms clasped behind his head as he waited for the phone to ring. He knew she was in the past, Sonya having informed him she had to jump forward to place the phone call.

3:45 struck and he took a deep breath, rapping his fingers on the desk, grabbing the computer's mouse to fidget with something. A grandfather clock stood in the opposite corner of the room, the seconds ticking away with the calming—yet torturous—sound of the pendulum swinging back and forth.

When 3:46 hit, Chris stared at the small clock on the lower right corner of his computer screen, the time teasing him. His legs started to bounce underneath the desk. "Where are you, Sonya?" he mumbled, turning on his cell phone's screen to ensure the time was consistent across all devices.

3:47 came and Chris scratched his head before letting his hand land over his mouth. He pinched his lips as his eyes remained fixated on the time, the minutes seeming to drag.

At 3:48 he unlocked his cell phone and scrolled through his past calls until he found the one time-stamped from last week at 3:45. The caller ID showed as "Unavailable", but he pressed on it to see where it might ring, bracing for Sonya to answer. It rang fifteen times before Chris hung up and dropped the cell phone on top of his desk, standing up to pace around the office. "Sonya, this isn't funny," he said to the phone, refusing to break eye contact with it.

By the time the clock struck 3:50, Chris started grabbing loose items on his desk and hurling them at the walls, cursing under his breath.

He picked up his cell phone and dialed again, faced with the same response. "What the *fuck*?" he asked the empty office, sitting back down and letting his legs continue their antsy bouncing.

He called Duane, who didn't answer. He called Mario Webster down at Wealth of Time, who also did not answer—his call went straight to voicemail. The thought crept into his mind that this was the moment Briar had planned for. Alone in his office, he'd have no way of knowing if time was frozen, so he opened the door and trudged into the living room, relieved at the sight of his soldiers gathered around the TV, laughing at a stand-up comedy special of Louis C.K.

Chris grumbled before returning to his office relieved to know it wasn't time to fight, but panic further bubbling within.

65

Can she actually be hurt? he wondered. *Yes, but there are plenty of other logical reasons she hasn't called—no need to panic. She could have fallen asleep for an afternoon nap. Could be out at the store and lost track of time. Or maybe she just forgot. She does have the tendency to be a bit scatterbrained at times.*

"Or she's in trouble," Chris said, his voice drowning out his internal thoughts.

His legs had grown tired from the constant bouncing and pacing, and he reached down to rub them, not yet realizing he hadn't done that in over forty years. Chris considered a couple of options at this point, and debated infiltrating the Road Runners' network, just to spark some life into them and see if he could get a reaction from their commander. A sensation kept gnawing in his gut that something was indeed off about this entire situation, but he kept ignoring it. Perhaps he was still too high from his slaughter of Thaddeus to grasp such negative thoughts. Maybe he refused to believe that his life would ever actually be in danger. Whatever the reason, Chris would soon realize he had made a mistake by not listening to—and trusting—his instincts.

He decided to go straight to the source and dialed Martin Briar. Like everyone else in the world, apparently, the call headed straight to voicemail. Chris declined to leave a message and hung up, glaring across the room to the grandfather clock that rang its dull bell four times to signify four o'clock had arrived.

The reality finally sunk in that Sonya was not calling, and for a rare instance, Chris Speidel had no idea what to do. He didn't want to rush into any drastic conclusions, but the phone calls had a purpose for his well-being.

With Revolters all around the country, Chris returned to his computer and put out an email blast to all offices, calling for every single member to find Sonya. It would take a couple hours for the messages to be relayed and put into action, especially considering each team would decide how to best spread their members both across time and locations. He'd expect to hear some sort of results within four hours, meaning he had to hunker down in this house under full security, just in case.

Once the email was sent, Chris powered off his computer and barged into the living room. "We have a situation," he explained to his soldiers, who promptly turned off the TV and gathered around. "I have not heard from Sonya for our regularly scheduled phone call. I don't have reason to believe my life is in jeopardy, at the moment, but I want to exercise caution. We need to completely secure the perimeter of the property. I want all of you to get into position outside and shoot anything that approaches—we have no expected visitors. I'll be in my office and will keep my weapons nearby. Stand your ground until I inform you it's safe to retreat inside."

As usual, his soldiers didn't question anything and silently moved about the house to grab their rifles and coats before strolling outside for the next few hours. With the house empty, Chris returned to the office and locked the door, closed the windows and blinds, and retrieved the pistol from his desk drawer. He lay on the couch, hoping to pass the time until hearing from someone.

Chris never felt the fatigue or sleepiness creep into his head. Sure, he had slept at night to pass the quiet hours, but he never expected to fall into a deep afternoon nap that his body demanded. His mind drifted away and took him under, into the first natural sleep cycle since becoming the Keeper of Time. While he snoozed, Chris never felt the grumbling in his stomach or the dryness filling his mouth as he fully returned to a somewhat regular, vulnerable, human being.

Chapter 10

A pending disaster was well underway by the time the Council returned from their lunch break and resumed their daily session. Their calendar had been filled with minor matters to settle, but that was all pushed aside when news broke about the assassination of Thaddeus Hamilton.

At first, the story was nothing but shock for the Road Runners, many of them grateful that Chris had actually attacked someone else besides them. That factoid, however, sparked a wave of panic throughout the membership that the organization was not ready for.

Many considered it a warning shot. If Thaddeus could be killed, why not Commander Briar? And where was he, anyway? The Council's email inbox had flooded with requests regarding their commander's whereabouts. As rocky as the election and transition from Strike to Briar had been, many had rallied behind Martin yet still had a rotten taste in their mouths having watched the gruesome death of Strike.

The news had broken just before the Council recessed for lunch, and by the time they came back an hour later, a crowd of roughly thirty Road Runners had gathered in the marketing office upstairs, demanding protection from the organization as they grew convinced of pending mayhem.

Chief Councilman Uribe ordered security members upstairs to gauge what exactly the members wanted.

"Our time of reckoning has arrived!" one member shouted. "Our war ends tonight!"

The crowd cheered these statements as truths, despite no one having any evidence to back it up.

Word leaked back to the Council as they convened for the afternoon and what was sure to be a long night ahead.

"Have we heard from the commander and his team?" Uribe asked Councilman Bolt, who had been tasked with reaching out to the team working on the Depression-era mission.

"We have not, sir, and I'm concerned. Because of the nature of this mission, we've had three checkpoints scheduled throughout the day, each and every day since they left. We last heard from Lieutenant Commander Herrera this morning, confirming that they were going into Sonya's apartment today. It's now been ninety minutes since their last check-in was due."

"And have we checked the tracking system?"

"Yes, sir, they all still appear to be in Chicago—in the same building—alive and well. That's why we're not quite concerned about them yet. The mission could have hit some bumps—they expected as much dealing with Sonya."

Uribe took off his glasses and tossed them on the table, rubbing his eyes and forehead, just as the head of security, Devin Janae, barged into the chambers with her eyes bulging.

"I'm sorry to interrupt, but we have a situation," she said, approaching the Council's table, but staying back a couple feet.

"We already know what's brewing upstairs," Uribe said, hoping that Devin's announcement wasn't anything more than that.

70

"No, sir. It's that, but there's more. Similar gatherings are happening all around the continent right now. I've received calls from Mexico City, Atlanta, Vancouver, and lots more."

"Shit," Uribe said. "I need to address the organization. Can we arrange a video call upstairs? I'd like to show us interacting with one of these crowds so they don't think we're just cowering."

Commander Briar had implemented a stronger push for transparency between leadership and the members, but not a total barrage of information. For example, Uribe could share that the commander was currently working on a secret mission, but not give any details. No one pushed back against this initiative as many believed it would alleviate random visits to the office from members, and hopefully cut down on their email inboxes. Both of those wishes had gone out the window today, more emails and members piling up.

"Head up in ten minutes," Devin said, and bolted out of the room.

"I would like to tell our members that their commander is indeed okay," Uribe said, returning his attention to the Council. "Keep making those calls—try every name we have listed on the mission sheet until someone answers. We need an answer in the next ten minutes."

"Do you think we need to authorize any special protections?" Councilwoman Dawson asked.

"I think that may be premature."

"I disagree," Councilwoman Barns chimed in. "When have you ever heard of this sort of thing happen across the continent? We're a few minutes away from a potential point of no return. We need to mitigate any threats or violence immediately."

"Our people don't do stuff like that," Uribe said.

71

"With all due respect, sir, times have changed since you last mingled with the general public," Barns said, all six heads snapping around to look at Uribe's reaction.

He stared blankly at his Council, unsure of what exactly to say. He wanted to argue the point, but he had certainly paid attention to the ever-changing dynamic of the organization. New members came in less concerned about building wealth, and more focused on how to use their unique talents to make the world a better place. And that required pushback against the norm. It hadn't blindsided Uribe, per se, but he never realized that the former minority had now become the majority within the Road Runners, pressing forward with their cause, demanding accountability from the organization.

"We're at a crossroads," he said. "And it seems like we have been at a new one every week for the past three months. It's apparent that we are headed in a different direction as an organization—the landscape has shifted so much since I first joined. Maybe I've overstayed my welcome on this Council, maybe my vision for the Road Runners is too archaic for where we're headed. But I've got to see us make it through these growing pains. I appreciate you putting me in my place, Barns—that took a lot of guts. That's exactly what it takes to rise to my seat in these chambers, and quite frankly, to have a long successful career as a Councilor. Don't ever stop standing up for what you believe in, and always speak your mind. I'm going to head upstairs and face the music. Hopefully I can resolve this, but some issues are starting to appear too big for us to reel in. No matter how ugly it gets out there, remember we have each other in these chambers."

Uribe stood from the head of the table and left the room in a stunned silence. He knew his days were counting down until retirement from the Council—he probably would have done it already had former Councilwoman Murray not committed treason. He had to leave the next generation of councilors with the best example he could—that was his sole responsibility at this point in time.

Uribe stomped through the office, turning a few curious heads, but was mostly ignored as he worked his way toward the stairs that led up to the marketing office. He went for quiet walks outside during the middle of the downtown lunch rush on weekdays, his preferred moments of alone time, despite having a guard ahead and trailing him every step. This trip upstairs, however, added extra weight on his shoulders, his feet dragging through the mud of anticipation.

When he reached the upper level and the private manager's office, he was greeted by Devin, her tattooed arms crossed as she paced around the room.

"Everything ready for me?" Uribe asked.

"Yes, sir," she replied. "We've set up the podium, cameras, and created a perimeter to keep the crowd at a safe distance. We also locked the building doors in case anyone passing by notices the crowd and tries to walk in."

"How many are inside?"

Devin shrugged. "We counted about fifty, but more kept coming in."

"Aren't there rules about how many can be in here at once?"

"Not up here. As far as going downstairs, no one is allowed any more without an appointment. Upstairs has become a sort of waiting room for Road Runners wanting to talk to leadership."

"I see, well let's get started."

Devin nodded and opened the office door, a flood of white

noise from the crowd blasting into the room. She led Uribe down a short hallway, passing a couple other office doors until they reached the main bullpen and lobby where at least 100 people stood jammed behind a roped-off area. Devin continued forward, standing ten feet in front of the podium where she would face the crowd during Uribe's speech.

Uribe stepped up to the microphone, took a sip from the glass of water on the podium's top shelf, and tapped the mic. "Good afternoon, Road Runners," he said, pausing to let the noise quiet down, all eyes in the room piercing into his soul.

"Where is Commander Briar?" a voice shouted from the crowd, followed by a steady murmur from others.

Uribe raised his hands. "Thank you all for coming out here today. I understand similar movements are happening around the continent, so I wanted to take the opportunity to come talk to not just this room, but all Road Runners watching on TV.

"First off, Commander Briar is currently on a mission. Before you ask, we cannot offer any details. Last our team heard this morning, everything is going as planned and the Commander is doing well."

"Is it a mission to get Sonya?" someone asked.

"Like I said, we cannot give any details regarding the mission. He is our commander, and that information must remain confidential. Now, I can assure you the mission does involve potential steps to end the war with the Revolution. While we appreciate everyone's eagerness to get things done, I need you to understand this is a process. Commander Briar has been working since day one to end this war, and the pieces have gradually been falling into place. This current mission is another step in the right direction."

"We're done waiting!" a man in the front shouted. "We'll

go get Chris and Sonya ourselves. We've had enough sitting around in fear, waiting for you all to get something done."

This earned a raucous roar from the crowd, many fists pumping in the air to mix with the commotion of whistles and shouting. The man turned to face the crowd, his back to Uribe. "We don't need permission, and we certainly don't need any help. Let's end this war ourselves. Once and for all!"

The room howled as Uribe banged the podium, but his call for attention was drowned out by the mob.

"Everybody calm down!" Uribe boomed into the mic, but he had lost all control over the room. Several of the other guards in the building had gathered around, forming a line at the rope barrier separating the visitors from Uribe.

"On my lead!" the man shouted, people parting to clear a path as he marched toward the exit.

"Cut the feed!" Uribe howled to Devin. "Cut it now!"

Devin obliged, but it was too late. Uribe wanted to prevent the rest of the continent from seeing the situation unfold.

"Oh God," Uribe whispered to himself as the crowd filed out of the building, chanting and hollering as they marched through downtown Denver, not caring if anyone from the general public saw them. "This is bad."

Uribe left the podium and started back for the chambers downstairs, needing to place an urgent call to the commander, but unable to because no one had yet to hear from him.

Chapter 11

When Uribe entered the chambers he found each Councilor on their cell phone, some remaining at the table, others tucked into corners of the room for added privacy. Devin walked with him, on a call of her own as reports spilled in from around the continent following the scene in Denver.

Councilwoman Dawson had remained at the table and hung up her phone. "We're calling everyone on the mission sheet—no one's answering. We're about to start calling them back a second time."

"Do we think they're in any danger?" Uribe asked.

"We don't have any tips that suggest they're in trouble, but the fact that we can't get ahold of anyone is troubling."

"Do we have any eyes on Chris Speidel?"

"We do not, no one has seen him since the Hamilton murder."

"Okay, keep calling, and I'm gonna see what's happening in the rest of the world."

Dawson wasted no time and dialed another number.

"What's the word?" Uribe asked Devin, who had remained by his side with urgency on her face.

"It's bad, sir. Similar marches ensued right after the one here. We're following the progress of twenty different marches through the tracking software. I'm worried this is the end of the road for our secret. There's no way the general public won't inquire what's going on."

"You'd be surprised. There have been plenty of instances in the past like this, and people just drive by. Or they'll check the news, see no headlines about the crowds, and just continue with their lives."

"But never this widespread, right?"

Uribe sighed. "Correct, and that's what worries me. They're not going to government buildings are they? *That* would be the end of our secret."

"As of now, no reports of activity near any government buildings. The crowd here is just marching down the Sixteenth Street Mall. They're turning heads, but no one understands what's going. We suspect the same is happening around the continent."

"Okay, let's keep it that way. Wherever we have the resources, create a barrier to prevent any of these groups from getting too close to government buildings or media outlets. If we can do that, we'll be fine. Does your team have any insight regarding our commander's whereabouts?"

"I'm afraid nothing different than you have. We see him on the tracking software and know he's still in Chicago, and his heart is beating—same for everyone with him."

"Has there been any movement?"

"Yes, they've been moving around the building, but we're not able to really judge what any of it means. It's a multilevel complex and our tracking software can't decipher between different floors."

"Okay, we'll keep calling until someone picks up—they have to be leaving that era soon."

Devin put up a finger as her phone rang again and answered

it. Uribe took the opportunity to try Martin himself, hoping that seeing his name on the caller ID might alert him of the urgency.

"Sir, we have a problem," Devin said, stuffing her phone back into her pocket. "I want to see for myself. Can we turn on your TV?"

She nodded at the TV hanging on the back wall the chambers, rarely used by the Council.

"Be my guest," Uribe said, following Devin as she dashed across the room and turned on the TV. He watched as she flipped through the channels and turned up the volume, landing on a local news station.

An aerial view of the Sixteenth Street Mall showed the mob of people marching down it, chanting "The war ends tonight!" A man's deep voice spoke over the footage.

"Ladies and gentlemen, we appear to have a protest of some sort happening downtown right now. Officials are unsure what war the angry mob is yelling about, and calls for police have been made to maintain the peace. No violence or riots have been reported. This is a developing story."

The screen showed the crowd had already grown in size, at least 200 people following the crazed man who had just barged out of the marketing office. Devin flipped through all the local news stations, finding them each covering the mysterious march taking place down the block.

"We're fucked," Uribe said. "Tell your teams to leave any weapons behind. If we show up with guns, this will spiral even more out of control. Have them hold that perimeter, but don't interfere with any local law enforcement—that's a sure way to derail everything. Do we know if coverage has started in other parts of the continent?"

"Haven't received word on that yet, but I'm sure it's a matter of time. Some of these crowds are over 300 people strong."

"Okay, let's make arrangements for a blackout across the continent, and I'll convene the Council right now to get a formal vote on the matter. I hope it's not necessary, but I don't want to take any chances since both of our *leaders* are missing."

"Yes, sir." Devin nodded and left the chambers, phone already to her ear as she fielded yet another call.

"Order in the chambers!" Uribe yelled, demanding silence from everyone. They hung up their phones and returned to the table where their chief had already settled back into his seat. "Do we have any updates?"

They all looked around blankly, silent.

"First off, I want none of you to panic. We have procedures in place for just about any situation you can think of, even this one. It is up to myself as the Chief Councilor to declare a state of emergency in the absence of both the commander and their lieutenant. The Bylaws state if reasonable attempts to make contact with leadership have failed, the Council will act on a temporary basis until they are heard from. I'd say we've reached that point, so I'm calling to vote a blackout for the Road Runner organization."

"That seems drastic," Councilman Bolt said.

Uribe raised a hand. "It is, but we can't sit on our hands. Unfortunately, this matter is too widespread for us to contain through regional means. We need to take control over the entire continent, and this will be a short, three-hour blackout—in which time we better hear something back from Chicago."

"Can you remind me what exactly a blackout entails?" Councilman Roth asked. "I'm familiar with the gist of it, but not all the details."

"Yes. A blackout calls for the shutdown and closure of all Road Runner offices around the continent. The doors will be locked and the power will be cut off for the duration of the blackout. This prevents anyone from entering or exiting our buildings thanks to our electronic locks. We offer a twenty-minute notice to all offices in case anyone needs to be outside, but we strongly encourage they remain inside for safety concerns. A blackout also cuts the feed for our network. All communication will be handled via direct text messages to our members. It also calls for all Road Runners who live outside of an office to remain inside their homes and urge any friends or family to do the same. All of this is done to allow our security teams the freedom to focus on the unraveling issue without having to worry about potential threats to our offices and members. It doubles our number of guards to help contain the situations brewing across the land as we speak. I will put up the three-hour blackout for a vote. It must be voted on and approved each time we wish to extend it, should it come to that. The commander reserves the right to call off the blackout, but we must inform him of the situation first. Please cast your votes and place in the box."

Uribe gestured to their ballot box sitting on the table and waited as everyone scribbled their vote on small slips of paper.

Once all votes were cast, he pulled in the box and immediately started opening the papers and keeping a tally. "Reminder, we only need a majority vote to pass any emergency actions."

His eyes bounced from the papers to his notepad where he drew a tally mark of each vote, passing the slips over to Councilman Bolt for confirmation.

"I count five votes to two in favor of the blackout," Uribe declared.

"Confirmed," Bolt said in a monotone.

"Perfect. I'll arrange a call to all Lead Runners in North America to inform them of this decision. Plan for the blackout to commence in twenty minutes. During that time, take the moment to gather any snacks and drinks you may need for the evening. Our role during all of this is to make preparations in the event neither of our leaders return."

Councilwoman Penny gasped at the opposite end of the table. "We're on CNN *and* Fox News." She held up her cell phone and scrolled between the front pages of both sites speculating what this random cult was doing around America.

"Close that and stop worrying. Our actions now will help us contain this. We are in recess until I return."

Uribe stood and left the chambers, returning to his office where he'd send out a blast email to all Road Runner offices around the continent. He asked all regions to send text messages to their local populations informing of the blackout. Uribe believed that members reacted better when having news delivered by their local leader instead of someone from the top of the organization.

It only took him a couple minutes to outline the details and hit send, prompting him to lean back in his office chair and draw a deep breath. Something in his gut told him that Commander Briar was indeed in danger.

Chapter 12

They boarded the jet in Chicago, not jumping back into the present day of 2020 until all were accounted for and seated. The mood was mixed, some people clearly ready to celebrate a successful mission, while those closest to Martin refrained from showing too much joy, knowing their leader was experiencing dark times of his own.

"I don't want anyone to worry about me," Martin told Alina. "I'll be fine, just like I've always been. Dealing with loss is the only constant in my life."

He took his seat along a window, head resting on the glass pane. There was no denying the success they had just achieved and what it meant as they readied to fly back across the country, but his chest remained a hollow pit. He looked around to perhaps the greatest crew ever assembled for a mission in the history of the Road Runners, and Martin envied them all.

Every single person on this mission had been driven by such a strong force to end the war. And while Martin could relate, he didn't have a lifetime of boiling rage pushing him like many others. Several of the younger members had grown up as Road Runners, their parents having become members several years prior to their birth. They had an acute focus on their roles. From day one, they were programmed to hate the Revolution and dedicate their lives to bringing them down.

What they had collectively achieved this morning was nothing short of a glass ceiling being shattered. They had grown used to the notion that the Revolution wielded all the power and that little could be done to stop it. Today, however, a wave of new change brewed on the horizon, one that would soon become a hurricane.

Once the flight took off and reached its cruising elevation, the party started as nearly everyone on board grabbed a drink from the bar and chatted in small huddles around the jet. Conversation and laughter filled the air, bringing a small grin to Martin's lips.

He watched as Alina mingled for a few minutes, sipping her glass of wine until she locked eyes with him and came over, sitting in the lounge chair across from him.

"Enjoying the festivities?" Martin asked, growing thirsty for a glass of scotch.

"I am. How are you holding up?" Aline took another sip and leaned back to relax.

"Lots of reflection since we left the apartment building. You know, they don't give us leaders a lot of time for that."

Alina chuckled. "Oh, I know. We are superheroes who just have to power through our days like everything is fine. Have you checked your cell phone since we arrived back in 2020?"

Martin shook his head. "I haven't turned it on yet. It's been a nice couple of weeks being mostly out of the loop."

"Well, just so you know, there is a situation, but we have to keep focused on this mission—it's almost done."

Martin dropped his head back. "Please tell me it's not as bad as I think."

"It's not—it's actually about us. The Council voted for a

blackout across the continent until they hear back from anyone on our team. I've already informed the entire team to handover any communication devices they have."

"Why? That seems like an overreaction."

"Thaddeus Hamilton has been killed by Chris, along with three other Liberation leaders. He killed them all in Thad's house. We're not sure what exactly unfolded to make that happen—maybe Chris has fully lost his mind. But it all led to some serious panic by our members and they started flooding the offices around North America, demanding action. When Uribe wouldn't tell the people where you were, they stormed out of the offices and are now marching in the streets."

Martin leaned forward, scratching his head and rubbing his temples. "Jesus Christ," he whispered. "I'm going down as the worst commander in history, aren't I?"

"Don't be so hard on yourself. Look at where we're flying right now. On our way to Nevada to admire the destruction of Wealth of Time, then to make the final move on Chris. Sure, you've dealt with a carousel of external issues, but no commander has ever been in this position. And keep in mind, we have *always* been at war—that's literally *why* our organization exists. It may not feel like it, but you're on the verge of becoming the *greatest* commander of all time."

Martin stared blankly and forced a half smile from the corner of his mouth. "Are we sure this is the right thing to do—not communicating with the Council?"

"It's not that big of a deal, in my opinion. They might be overreacting right now, but if we show up tonight with Chris Speidel's dead body, then no one will even remember the last twenty-four hours of this mess. These marches will turn into dancing in the streets."

"I understand—I just don't want anything reflected badly upon us. It seems almost childish to intentionally not check in with our own organization."

"Last I looked, our job descriptions aren't to check in with people. It's to protect this organization to the best of our abilities. And that's exactly what we're doing. Now is not the time to dwell and question every decision we've made. It's time to meet our fate and look it square in the eye, especially you. This entire mission falls into your hands once time is frozen. Martin and Chris, good versus evil—not another soul to interrupt."

"Gee, thanks for the added pressure." Martin laughed and turned to look at the team still celebrating, oblivious to the dark road ahead for their commander. "Must be nice to feel that sense of accomplishment like they are. I've been chasing that my whole life."

"You'll find it soon enough. On that note, are you ready to discuss the next steps?"

Martin had a rough idea how the rest of the night would play out, but many of the details remained within Alina's plans. He had wanted to make sure they actually reached this point before occupying his mind with more worry. With Sonya dead, he could no longer avoid the pending task that fell squarely upon his shoulders.

"Okay, what do we have?" he asked, begrudgingly pulling out a small bottle of water from the side flap on his seat. He had made a personal vow to not drink in front of other Road Runners, except for Alina. Too many eyes were present and he had a reputation to uphold.

"I have confirmation that Chris returned to Idaho after killing Thaddeus. Now, it's expected to be heavily guarded, so we have

85

to plan exactly when we want Steffan to freeze time. We expect some serious backlash from Commander Blair for not being told that this is happening, so the less time the better. There are still some unknown factors. Once time is frozen, we don't know how Chris will react. Will he stay put and fight from his house? Get in the car and drive away? Does he know how to fly a plane? Because that can make things complicated."

"We need to keep eyes on him the entire time," Martin added. "I don't know how he's done it in the past, but he's been able to somehow enter my mind and see where I am. Would hate for him to start running before we even arrive."

"I wouldn't count on that happening. We've done our homework on the Keeper of Time ability and how it works—it's all in the blood. Chris is growing weaker by the minute. See, the Keeper blood isn't meant to last forever. Past Keepers have died at a normal age after stepping down from their role. The blood itself is not what makes them invincible; contrary to public belief, it's the presence of that blood in another living being that keeps the Keeper from dying. So even if Sonya hadn't died today, she'd just keep aging and eventually pass away, deeming that injection of Keeper blood in her system useless."

Martin nodded, drinking his water as he grew entranced by the lesson.

"What's happening right now has never happened before, at least from the Keeper history we've been able to research. Chris's body had always been aging, even as the Keeper, but his invincibility and other abilities have not. Our team of hematologists believe that his body is going through a sort of catch-up period. Think of Sonya as a dam holding everything together: invincibility, special powers, natural time travel abilities to name a few. Her death is the breaking of that dam and now everything is 'catching up' or regressing to match Chris's current age—which we believe is right around 100 years old. The very blood in his system is now eroding to match that age, just like it would a regular human man. With that erosion goes his powers. If nothing changes by the time we arrive to Idaho, it's very possible that Chris won't even be able to travel through time by sheer will like he used to."

"Well, that would make this all a lot easier," Martin said with a laugh.

"It would. He won't be able to enter your mind, won't be able to jump through time. He'll just be a fragile old man you have to hunt down and put the final nail in his coffin." Alina grinned as she said this last part.

"There is no way it's that simple."

"But it is—that's why there's been the sudden push for Sonya's life. These findings have been gradually coming along for the past five years. Combine that with Chris's age, and the window has opened for this opportunity. Getting Sonya was the hard part, but she threw us a bone. I wonder if she knew all of this?"

Martin didn't want to discuss or speculate about Sonya. Not yet. "If I know Chris, he has plans in place for this exact scenario already. The guy plans every single detail and prepares for all possibilities, even the ones we might consider impossible."

"You're probably right. And he's in amazing shape despite his appearance. He moves around just fine and will likely make a run to save his life."

"Do we know what weapons he has access to? I'm ready for a shootout, but who knows with him."

"We don't know for sure, but suspect there are fewer unique

weapons at his disposal in his new house. Destroying his mansion was so crucial to all of this, too. We got him out of his safe space and away from what was certainly a bunker full of weapons from the past and future. And keep in mind, this reality is going to hit Chris at some point—it may already have. Once he realizes he's mortal, expect rushed decisions and scrambling. He may inject the nearest person he finds with his blood as a desperate attempt to save himself, but that process typically takes a few hours until it actually works. This is why you're going to kill every Revolter on his property, even while they're frozen. We can't afford any gambles."

"You want me to shoot frozen statues?"

"Think of it as target practice and you'll be fine. Hey, if they weren't frozen they'd be shooting at you, so it's all justified."

"You amaze me."

"I know. Once you kill them, it's a matter of hide-and-seek. Make sure you're not in a position to get shot while you work through his house. He's in the middle of absolutely nothing—not even trees to hide behind—so we don't expect him to run on foot. Slash the tires of any vehicles on the property and guarantee he doesn't leave."

"And what if he has just enough power left to slip away?"

"That won't happen. We have eyes on him. A team is set up about five miles away from his house. They have drones, cars, a helicopter, and a single-engine airplane. We are ready for anything. We also have people planted in every year covering a 500-year period. Keep in mind, we are counting on a rushed decision, so none of this guarantees anything."

"And all of these people know to not make any contact with the Council?"

"None at all. This entire team is on the same page. Chris

dies tonight, and nothing will stop that from happening. They all understand the gravity of the moment and everyone is committed to seeing it through the finish line."

"I feel better about letting the phone ring off the hook."

"Yeah, and we should be fine with the blackout, too—I'd say that actually works in our favor. I was worried they'd send people once they saw our tracking devices moving together, but they can't unlock the buildings to let people out, so now they're working with a limited pool of soldiers to deploy our way, less if they need them to contain the mess on the streets. And if they try to call off the blackout earlier than planned, the membership will know something is going on and will add more fuel to the fire. The Council just handcuffed themselves."

"Okay, let's get this done. How much longer until we reach Nevada?"

"About another hour."

Martin nodded and returned his attention to the window, looking down to the world passing below, praying he'd be able to make it the peaceful place it deserved to be.

Chapter 13

Chris shot up from the couch, his head cloudy and spinning, his stomach feeling hollowed out. The sensations were familiar; that they were happening, told Chris all he needed to know. His sense of surrounding had evaporated during the nap—

—*a fucking nap?! Right now?!*—

—and he squandered around his office until holding his balance on the grandfather clock showing an entire hour had passed.

"Arrrgghhh!" he bellowed, grabbing the clock from the top and hurling it sideways, the clatter of metal echoing in the room as the pendulum, weights, and chains all collided with one another. "This isn't happening," he whimpered, dragging himself to his desk and fishing his pistol out of the top drawer, only to find that he already had it tucked into his belt. "What is *wrong* with me?" he asked the empty room, grabbing the sides of his head.

So much could have happened in the last hour, but his cell phone showed no alerts. He checked the Road Runner network and found it offline, creating a slow drip of paranoia that wouldn't go away for the rest of the night. He dialed Mario Webster, only to have the call go straight to voicemail. He tried Sonya again with the same result, rage and fear boiling within, the sensation similar to nausea for regular human beings, considering he fed off the two emotions.

Chris looked out the window to see his team of soldiers in their positions, scattered about the property just as he had instructed. If no one was going to answer his calls then he'd need to visit them in person. The closest place was the Wealth of Time store only 100 miles southwest.

He trudged out of the office and stepped outside, barking his next commands. "We need to get on the jet right now!"

The soldiers moved without a word, all of them rotating to different positions to ensure coverage on the grounds, the three soldiers who accompanied Chris on trips quickly loading their weapons into the van, one holding a door open for the Keeper of Time as he made his way to join them.

"Colin, we're landing the jet back here at the house on our way back, do you understand?"

"Yes, sir," said the stony-faced man, waiting for Chris to get in the van.

"I'm done with this ridiculous hour-long drive to the hangar. We may not have much time tonight in case we need to run."

"Yes, sir."

They piled into the van and hit the road, the jet an hour away, Wealth of Time only a thirty-minute flight from there.

*　*　*

Chris wrestled reality as they flew to northern Nevada, even though it stared him square in the face. His stomach growled, mouth turning into cotton. If he ate food and drank water—something he'd never done in front of his soldiers—would that display of weakness affect their ability to work for him? He debated this with much ferocity, perhaps overthinking the matter. Perhaps not. His mind wasn't right and he could only assume it was because of his body's demands. All of this only meant one thing, too.

There's no way Sonya is dead, he thought. His stomach groaned in protest. *Why? How? I should have never let her leave. This is life and death, and I let my only insurance policy walk away.*

He had no time to dwell on the past. Martin would make his move tonight, guaranteed. Chris wanted to rush to Wealth of Time, not to see Mario and inquire why none of his calls were being answered, but to inject his blood into his longtime confidant and trusted advisor. It might not guarantee anything, but if Chris could stay off the grid for at least twenty-four hours he'd have the chance to recuperate his abilities and truly ready himself for a fight with the Road Runners.

He needed answers on Sonya, the whereabouts of Martin Briar, why the Road Runners were offline, and why the hell no one was answering their phones.

The jet prepared for its descent not much longer after it had taken off. It rumbled as they dropped, and Chris felt what might have been fear for the first time in almost half of a century.

The store had been deliberately located to allow for flights in and out directly next to it, a landing strip stretching a mile into the distance, surrounded by a decorative row of cacti. The landing was smooth and they eased to a complete stop.

"Sir, we have a situation," Colin's voice crackled through the speakers.

Chris felt his gut drop, another sign that things were definitely far from normal. He wasn't ever supposed to be nervous, in full control over his life and fate. There was no time for surprises, but this day continued to unravel before his eyes.

He pushed his way to the cockpit, glancing out the window to a pile of charred wood and ash. His chest tightened at the sight, and for a moment he thought he might be having a heart attack, until he realized his entire body had tensed up. His lips parted, but no words came out. For perhaps the first time in his life, Chris Speidel had no idea what to say.

A body lay on the ground, roughly thirty feet away from the rubble that was once the entrance to Wealth of Time.

"Let's get out there!" Chris howled, his team whipping into shape and marching down the stairs that folded out from the jet. Chris followed, his legs wavering as they grew tired with each step.

The jet had stopped roughly 100 feet away, a distance that seemed an eternity as Chris dragged himself toward the body on the ground. When he approached, he found Mario still conscious, blood oozing from his abdomen in a silent stream. His eyes locked on Chris, and the faintest of smiles touched his lips.

"Mario?" Chris asked, kneeling down and placing a hand on his friend's chest.

"They found us," Mario wheezed, his voice much stronger than Chris expected, as the man appeared minutes from death.

"The Road Runners did this?"

Mario nodded in a slow, painful motion. He hadn't moved so much as a finger, his body becoming a vegetable in the middle of the desert.

"They killed us all," Mario said. "Twenty of them showed up and started shooting. Then they set the place on fire. C-can you help me, Chris?"

93

Desperation dripped from every word that left Mario's lips, and Chris once more encountered the human emotions brewing within his chest. This time he felt sorrow. Mario had managed to survive a mass murder and arson attack, crawling for the slimmest chance of living beyond sunset.

Chris licked his lips, the taste of fear and death emanating strongly from his friend. Even someone he had known most of his life was not exempt from satisfying Chris's hunger, especially under these new circumstances where Chris couldn't quite decipher which hunger was gnawing at him more—the stomach or the soul.

He looked to the ground where the pool of blood beneath Mario's body had already started to dry and harden. The man had been lying out here for at least an hour, which meant the Road Runners carried out this attack while Chris slept in his Idaho home. *And that's why we're built to resist the basic needs of the human body.*

"Mario, my dear friend," Chris said. "I don't think you're going to make it. We've had a hell of a run, you and I. Thanking you would be an understatement. Are there any matters you'd like me to handle in your death?"

"Just run, Chris. And hide."

These would be the final words spoken in Mario Webster's life. His eyes glossed over as he gazed to the crisp blue sky above. Within hours that same sky would turn black as the Revolution faced their ultimate test.

Chris brushed his fingers over Mario's eyes to close them and grunted as he rose to his feet. He shuffled to the remains of his infamous store. Decades of memories, rare art and collectibles, and his state-of-the-art laboratory were now crumbled remains of history. The air became still as Chris had a moment of silence in front of the building, the stench of burnt wood prominent.

They had to have covered the entire storefront with kerosene or some other flammable firestarter for the entire thing to have burned down within an hour. With enough people, that wouldn't have been an issue, especially if they had no resistance from the Revolters who called this place home.

Though he had many accomplishments during his reign as the Keeper, the Wealth of Time store was by far his favorite. All Keepers responded differently to their dose of the sacred blood. Some facets were universal, like the ability to jump through time by simply thinking of it. And of course, the guarantee of invincibility by injecting one's own blood into a trusted source.

A handbook of sorts was kept as the Keeper status was passed down, where each new Keeper suggested to try some of the abilities that had been learned by their predecessors, and recorded any new findings. No one had ever logged the ability to read minds, something that seemed to come and go at times for Chris.

What sparked the idea for the storefront, however, was an ability called "mirroring", something first discovered and only used by an old Keeper of Time from the late-1700s. Keepers dealt with bending the dimension of time, but that sometimes became intertwined with other dimensions as well. Mirroring allowed a Keeper to project and reflect real life images to a different location. Wealth of Time always stood in this private location, desolate in the northern Nevada desert to never be found. Mirroring allowed Chris to recreate this same store as an illusion all around the continent, using it as a means to lure in potential recruits—and even casual passersby. Anyone who walked through those doors was fair game.

The idea had been well received by those in leadership positions, and Chris even fulfilled some requests for different types of buildings to reach other demographics of people—not everyone had interest in visiting antique shops. This all led to the most successful recruitment efforts ever implemented in the world of time travel. He could "construct" a new building within minutes and have it torn down just as fast, leaving people in the area puzzled as to what the hell had happened. In time, he learned to perform this in remote areas that wouldn't attract as much attention and lead to speculation from the regular citizens of the continent.

Chris no longer could perform this once simple task. His special powers had grown into a sixth sense, something he could call upon without much effort. Now, a hole had formed in his soul where these abilities once were. All of his powers escaped from his body like a silent, gradual leak of air from a tire.

He closed his eyes, needing to test for good measure, and thought of the year 2000, squeezing all the effort from his brain to take him back to that year when life had been much simpler.

Nothing happened.

When he opened his eyes and saw the demolished Wealth of Time, it finally occurred to Chris that his chances of winning this battle against Martin were dwindling by the second. He had no one to turn to for safekeeping his blood, no way to dodge the trouble facing him by jumping around time.

"They did it," he whispered. "After all these years, they finally found a way to isolate me."

He had plans for this situation. They weren't ideal, considering his age and depleting body, but he'd never go down without a fight, especially against Martin Briar.

"Let's get back on the jet, gentlemen," he said to his team waiting behind him. "I have to grab some things, then we'll be off again. We have a long night ahead, so I suggest you all rest up."

Chris led the way, his soldiers marching behind him, leaving behind Wealth of Time forever.

Chapter 14

Of all the plans he had for every unthinkable situation that could arise, this one was perhaps the most simple.

"We're flying directly to the house," Chris reiterated once on the jet. "I need about ten minutes inside then we'll be off. Just me and Colin—no one else. I can't travel with a crew anymore. Colin, once we arrive to our final destination, you'll be free to leave. I'll be in touch when I'm ready for a flight back home, but that might take weeks."

"Yes, sir," Colin said before disappearing into the cockpit.

Everyone took their seats, Chris off to the side for privacy away from his soldiers. The day had turned him into a child, experiencing particular emotions and events for the first time, at least as far as he could remember. He couldn't help but sulk.

The destruction of Wealth of Time was more than symbolic for Chris. The store served as an unofficial pillar for the entire Revolution. It had become their main source for recruitment, but more importantly, housed the laboratory responsible for producing over ninety-five percent of the Juice currently in circulation. Chris had refined the process for making Juice, perfecting it to a fine science that anyone could follow. That was why he left Mario in charge of the store and Juice production, a huge load off his shoulders that started shortly after he recruited Martin Briar.

With one of their pillars destroyed, Chris snapped out of his false denial, and now understood the future of the Revolution rested solely in his hands. A decades-long chess match now saw the Road Runners in a position to call check. For Chris, he was down but not out. And would never rollover.

"I need everyone to fasten their seat belts," Colin said over the intercom. "Expect a rocky landing."

Everyone obliged, including Chris, who didn't normally take precautions. He was in no position to take needless gambles.

The jet started its descent, and Chris watched out of his window, his house a small blip in the distance. The lone road near the house was their best option for landing. Chris understood just fine that they had no business landing on the deserted highway on a regular basis, but now was a special occasion that required it.

The jet approached the ground, hovering without committing to touching down, slightly wavering as it seemed Colin was hesitating. After ten more seconds, the wheels touched and everyone in the plane jerked forward, rattling and rumbling heard from the back pantry and bar.

They came to a gradual stop, parked a mere 100 yards away from the house. Orders had already been given, and all soldiers knew their assignments. Colin was to remain on the jet and keep it ready for the next leg of the trip. The stairs opened and Chris was the first one off the jet, jogging down the steps and toward his house.

Being human is awful, he thought, his century-old lungs begging for mercy by the time he reached the front door. All the soldiers who had remained behind were in the same exact positions from earlier.

"You're all free to return inside," Chris instructed from the front door. "Protect this house at all costs—I'll be back in a few weeks."

He pivoted inside without another word, heading straight for his office where he grabbed a duffel bag from the closet, already stuffed with cash, guns, and ammunition—all any human needed to survive, in Chris's opinion. He caught a glimpse of the jet through the office window and wondered if he'd ever return to this place. Sure he hated it, but it was one of the few things remaining that he could call his own.

Room had been intentionally left in the duffel bag in case Chris needed to throw in any last-minute items. He rummaged through his desk drawers and found a framed picture of him with his late wife, Gloria, and a young Sonya—Angelina at the time—no older than eight years old. They all had the widest grins, having enjoyed the warm sunshine during their photoshoot in the local park. Life had been hard back then, but it was simple, something Chris longed for in this moment.

Sonya's innocent eyes caught his attention, joyous, youthful, and filled with a bright ambition that had never really waned. He had long forgotten the sensation of love, but knew if he could claim the emotion for anyone, it was certainly his little girl. He only hoped her death had been painless, and felt a tinge of guilt at the prospect of never finding out what happened.

"The circle of life," he said to the empty room. "Just like Martin Briar went his whole life without knowing what happened to his daughter. Now *he* wants to deliver that same verdict to *me*?! I'll be damned if I let him. As soon as this blows over, I will find out the truth!"

He stuffed the photo into the bag, his heart set on surviving this rough patch and getting the answers he deserved. After one final scan he departed the house and started his next jog—although slightly slower thanks to the duffel bag over his shoulder—back to the waiting jet.

He climbed the steps and never looked back as Colin closed the door, his pilot eager to get back into the cockpit.

"Still headed for Minnesota, sir?" Colin asked.

"Let's go."

Chris took his seat as Colin disappeared, the engines rumbling. He felt the fluttering of butterflies in his stomach, the unknown future waiting on the other side of this flight. As they soared into the air, Chris looked at how small the world below appeared, and took the time to reflect on his life.

He tried to remember the man he was before entering this new life, but that seemed a blank page in his memory. He could picture himself, but had no ability to draw actual memories and feelings from those days. He remembered working in the factories, driving home exhausted to where Gloria and Sonya awaited him for dinner. Sometimes he'd stop at the bar for a stiff drink to take the edge off. That had been his undoing, as that's where the Revolution first approached him.

He closed his eyes and could see their old house in Colorado Springs, the green lawn, manicured shrubbery, flapping American flag over the porch. They were poor, but didn't know it. Happiness had overpowered the importance of money, until he came into a small fortune.

The smells from the kitchen usually greeted him in the driveway, especially in the summer when all the windows were left open. Sonya always ran up and jumped into his arms the moment he stepped out of the car, one of the bright spots in his life that had seemed to run on a constant loop.

The jet reached its cruising elevation and Chris unbuckled his seat belt, reclining his chair all the way back. As if the pressure of the past few months hadn't been enough—plus his return to being an emotional human today—Chris wondered, for the very first time since becoming Keeper, if it was all worth it.

He had traded away his family and the only life he knew for a few thousand dollars and a promise for a lifetime of fortune. The decision might have been shallow on the surface, but Chris knew in his heart the reasons he made them, mostly for Sonya. He always longed for her to grow up wealthy, a proper, sophisticated young lady with the world at her fingertips. She'd go to the best schools and live wherever she wanted with her perfect husband and children. And it would all be thanks to Chris making a gut-wrenching decision that made it all possible.

Chris reached over and grabbed the onboard telephone. He wanted to try some phone calls one final time before landing, since he didn't know how the next few days would play out. He tried Sonya first, accepting that she was never going to answer his call again. When he received that confirmation, he hung up and immediately dialed Duane. It rang six times before the voicemail kicked in, and he decided to leave a message.

"Duane, my dearest friend. I hope this message finds you doing better than me. I'm currently on my way to Minnesota—it appears the time has come for this trip. I only wish you were by my side—you can always catch a flight and join me, should you please, but I'll bet you prefer to stay in Florida. Honestly, I wish it was me joining you. Perhaps I can take the first vacation of my life when this is all over and come visit, if you'll have me.

"I'm about ninety-nine percent sure Sonya is dead. I haven't heard from her and have been feeling emotions all afternoon. It's actually been quite weird to think about what would happen if the engines on this jet failed and we went down. I won't call it fear, but I feel *something* about the prospect.

"It's funny how quickly acceptance can settle in. Not once did I think this day would actually come, despite planning for it. I suppose plans are just our subconscious preparing for the inevitable. I like to think this trip is foolproof and will guarantee my survival, but I can't help but wonder, especially with how our good friend, Mr. Briar, has come after me so aggressively.

"I haven't told a soul this, but the thought of death has planted itself in my head and no matter what I do it stays there, lurching, waiting. In case anything bad happens, I wanted to thank you for all of your help over the years. We had a great run, and I suppose all things really do come to an end. It's funny—I remember when Chester told me how all Keepers reach a point during their reign where they know it's time to step away. I haven't felt that yet, even with everything going on. I still have so much to give and even more to do. I still dream of a world with no Road Runners, and I intend to see it happen. Don't be surprised if you see the news headlines coming up and wonder if the end of the world is coming—it's just me trying to push the Road Runners to the brink of insanity.

"I'm rambling and I'm sorry—it's been a long day. I hope we get the chance to talk again soon. Goodbye, my friend."

He hung up and leaned back in his seat. With nostalgia throbbing in his mind, Chris shook his head to clear his thoughts, needing to focus on the task of survival. He was in the air, headed for the most remote location he kept a property in the continental United States. He had a fighting chance, which is all he could ask for under the circumstances. Now he just needed to fight.

Chapter 15

"This is the most beautiful sight I've ever seen," Martin said as they stood in front of the pile of ashes that was once Wealth of Time. "Would it be mean to piss on what's left?"

Everyone cackled.

Since the store was only a twenty-minute flight away from Chris's home in Idaho, Martin had insisted they stop to see the wreckage before moving to the final leg of the mission. He hadn't seen the store since his last trip to the area with Gerald. Wealth of Time represented the death to those closest to Martin, and the amount of glee filling his chest nearly lifted him off the ground. He only wished he had been around to see its destruction firsthand.

"Hell of a job," he said to Arielle, who had remained next to Alina in the small cluster they had formed in front of the fallen property. "Your team executed this to perfection—I'll make sure they get the proper recognition and additional compensation they deserve."

"Thank you, sir. I dedicated this mission to Gerald, and I know everyone on the team took that to heart."

"This is pure justice. Does anyone else feel something in the air today? Things are actually going our way for once."

The team cheered and howled, and Martin grinned. The loss

of Sonya stung and hadn't worn off, but he managed to come to terms with it, not wanting to waste her sacrifice. If they actually managed to pull off the unthinkable and live in a world with no threats from the Revolution, he had plans to build a new headquarters and name it after Sonya. He figured it had always been her destiny to be the hero in this war against Chris, considering she had the direct tie to him. And it would still play out this way if everything continued to fall into place.

Martin felt obliged to deliver a speech in front of the de-stroyed Wealth of Time store, even if it was only to the couple dozen of team members that had been by his side since they left Denver two weeks ago. He stepped forward, feeding off their energy.

"We're doing it," he started. "Each and every one of you, and all the other team members across the country and time. *We* are doing it. Hold your heads up high and be proud of what has already been accomplished. Today is the most important day in our organization's history. We stand on the shoulders of those before us. Let us not forget the efforts and research they had already completed to make all of this possible. This has been a team effort spanning almost fifty years.

"I want you to take a moment and think about *why* you're here today. Really think about it. For me, I was a lost soul who just wanted life to end. I held out a false hope that maybe one day my daughter would return. Chris lured me in that day, in this very store. And you know what? It actually worked. I'll never take the credit away from Chris for allowing me the chance to learn the truth. I owe him that much, but it stops there. After that, he spun me into a world of lies, murdered my mother, and has forced me to live a life where I constantly look over my shoulder. I know all of our stories aren't identical, but there are plenty of similarities.

"I never wanted to be commander—sometimes I still don't. I felt forced into the election and had no clue how anything in this organization worked. I've had doubts about my ability to lead. Doubts regarding whether I've been used as some sort of pawn in this war. I don't know why I'm a Warm Soul. I'm just a regular guy from Larkwood who dragged myself through the work week, only to drown out my problems with drugs and alcohol. I'm no one special.

"What I've learned since becoming commander is that each and every one of you *is* special. My title gets me respect, but it is undeserved. You are all the real heroes in this organization. You're the ones who have dedicated your entire lives to this cause—I arrived late to the party.

"On the other side of the state border waits the final stop of our destiny. I don't know how it will play out—we might even fail. I don't want to assume anything. I have the distinct opportunity of closing this out by myself. And even if I succeed, I want to tell you now that all the credit belongs to you. I'll be the one on TV giving interviews, but it's *you* who made it happen. Give yourselves a round of applause for coming this far, and let's get back on that jet for Idaho."

The team erupted, shouting in the desert where no one else would hear them, alone in the world for this intimate moment with their leader.

Martin rejoined them, Alina stepping forward as she waved her cell phone in the air. "I recorded the whole thing—the organization deserves to see that speech after we kill Chris."

Martin laughed and felt tears welling in his eyes. Tears of joy, something he couldn't recall having ever experienced since Izzy's birth. The cheering had died down as the rest of the team started back for the jet. Martin looked back to the remains of the store one final time, filling his soul with the warmth it needed after an excruciating morning.

It's actually happening. Keep going.

They filed onto the jet and took their seats, Alina sitting next to Martin as she scrolled on her cell phone. "The situations are getting a bit out of control, Commander. Just thought you should know."

"How so?"

"Fortunately nothing has turned violent, but the numbers are growing and it's officially grabbing the attention of national news channels."

She held up her phone that showed the homepage of *USA Today,* the headline asking the simple question of: Who are they?

The image showed a middle-aged man bundled up for winter weather, his mouth wide open mid-shout. Several signs could be seen in the background, blurred out except for one that said *We've had enough!*

"What are they saying?" Martin asked. "I'm sure reporters have tried talking to them."

"The article says that the protesters have remained mum on what they're actually protesting. They have answered with questions or blanket statements that make no sense to anything happening in the world. The chants don't make sense, the demographics aren't telling of what is actually happening. The American media is having a tough time figuring this out. The governor of California has called in the National Guard to Los Angeles, where they estimate 15,000 people have converged onto Hollywood Boulevard."

Martin chuckled. "The National Guard?"

"I guess they feel things are rowdy—there's an energy from the crowd that feels rather hostile."

"I can't lie—I'm impressed. All these protests and no one has outed us, even by accident. We truly are dedicated to keeping our secret, even if we're marching through the country causing a scene."

"It's more than the United States. Mexico City is reporting similar protests, along with Toronto, Panama City, and San José."

Martin nodded. "We're fine, right? What would actually happen if the secret slipped out?"

Alina shrugged. "We don't know for sure. Tests were done in the 80s to see, but results were inconclusive. We approached random strangers and told them about time travel, just to see how they'd react. Some nodded and kept walking, some asked if we were on drugs. And others asked to join. I think if something this widespread were to leak today, most of society would call bullshit and form their own conspiracy theories regarding who the people protesting really are. Social media has actually made it quite easy for us to brush something like this under the rug. I'm sure we have teams right now already spinning the stories online to misdirect the general public. Hell, you can even claim it's all fake, and half the world will believe you. Unless someone sees something with their own eyes, who are they to argue the facts?"

"I didn't realize we even had a social media team."

"It's just the technology team. Obviously we don't have a presence online as an organization, but many of our members enjoy fitting into the regular world, blending in, just the way we like it."

"I see." Martin looked out his window, the sun starting to

set on this day that seemed like it would never end. They were already starting their descent into the small town of Three Creek, Idaho, nerves bubbling within his guts as the ultimate showdown loomed.

"Uh, Commander?" Alina said after having fallen silent while she returned her attention to her cell phone. "I just got word that Chris has fled the property."

"What?!" Martin jumped out of his seat, as if he could do something about this recent development.

"We've had eyes on the house all day—all week, in fact—just to make sure nothing changed. Apparently Chris had left earlier in the day and returned by landing his jet near the house. He ran inside for a couple of minutes before getting back on and taking off—this time with no one else on board besides the pilot."

"Do we know which way he went?"

"Kind of. Our team only had a single-engine plane so they couldn't keep up with the jet too well. He was heading north, and we had another team with a jet ready in Twin Falls to tail him. We have eyes on him again and they believe he's headed for Canada based on the trajectory of the flight so far."

"Dammit," Martin said through gritted teeth. "What can we do? I don't want to lose ground."

"Don't worry about that. Our team will tail him all the way to the North Pole if that's where he's going. Once he lands, we'll know exactly where and can make arrangements. We're already descending, so we might as well have a look around his property and wait until we get word. No point in flying around in circles if we don't know where we're going."

"How far behind is our team from Chris?"

"About ten minutes. Assuming they land at an actual airport

and not the middle of nowhere, we should be landing right behind."

Martin nodded. "Tell your team to shoot the pilot right when they land. That's an order. Do not let that pilot get back in the air."

"Yes, sir."

Martin called for attention on the jet, every head turning to him as he spoke from the front of his seat, Alina still seated beside him as she sent a text message on her phone.

"Everyone get comfortable—we're staying on the jet a little longer than originally planned. I'll explain once we land, but for now we need all of you to make sure your guns are loaded and get into your protective gear."

They all moved without question, returning to their seats. Martin saw Arielle shooting a glance over to Alina, trying to get a read on the situation, but failing. He fell back into his seat and leaned his head against the window, the day seeming to only get longer with each passing second.

Where are you hiding, Chris?

Chapter 16

Colin landed the jet in Angle Inlet, Minnesota, the northern-most point of the contiguous United States. Chris had a lifetime of scouting under his belt to find the perfect location for his ultimate hideout. Barrow, Alaska was remote, but it was still in the open, and once the Road Runners learned about the location, they had no issue building their own headquarters nearby.

Angle Inlet, however, was plenty different thanks to its official population of ninety residents. Chris owned a cabin in the thick of the woods, lacking any neighbors within a two-mile radius. The town sat in a unique geographic location, a peninsula in the Lake of the Woods, where the United States and Canadian borders were drawn in the water. Even though the town was part of Minnesota, one could only drive there needing to first pass through Canada, as the peninsula was attached to the mainland of the Great White North.

When Chris discovered this little secret on the map it im-mediately became his favorite location should he ever need to hide for his life. That time had come, and the wheels were in full motion for him to spend at least two weeks in the cabin, waiting for the Road Runners to give up their search.

Part of the original plan, unfortunately, was to leave either Duane or Mario in charge during his absence, considering cell phone reception was spotty and the cabin lacked an internet connection.

When they touched down, though, Chris wasn't worried about any of these small details. Instead, he fumbled through the first-aid kit stored on the jet and pulled out a syringe, sticking it into the puffy vein on the back of his hand, drawing blood out in a painful ceremony. He hadn't felt such physical pain since the day he had transformed into the Keeper of Time, and let out a heavy pant for breath when he finished, clutching his hand and rubbing the area before applying a bandage.

"Colin," he cried, the pilot appearing within seconds in the cockpit doorway. "I need you to do me a big favor."

"What is it, sir?" Colin's eyes danced around the jet, bulging at the sight of the syringe and the few drops of blood that had splattered onto the floor.

"As you know, I'm not okay right now—that's why we're here. I need to inject my blood into your body, and if I can hide out for at least forty-eight hours I know I'll be in the clear and back to normal. After we do this I want you to fly wherever you want and lock yourself inside until you hear from me. Do you think you can do that?"

"Anything for the Revolution, sir." Colin offered an aggressive nod as he spoke.

"I appreciate that, as does the entire organization. Just so we're clear, you should not discuss this with a single soul. If anyone finds out we did this, the Road Runners will be after you. And if they killed Sonya, then they'll have no thoughts about sparing you."

"Understood, sir."

"Perfect." Chris stood up and gestured with his arm for Colin to sit down in his seat. "Roll up your sleeve and relax. It's just like any shot, and won't have any lasting pain." Colin sat down and did as instructed, taking a deep breath when Chris waved the syringe full of his own blood in the air.

"You're our last hope," Chris said moments before poking the needle into Colin's arm. He pushed all the blood out and removed the needle with the ease of a nurse who had done the same routine dozens of times each day. "I suggest you wait about ten minutes to make sure your body doesn't have any sort of reaction. It shouldn't, but it's good to be safe. I'd hate to go through this just for you to fall asleep at the wheel and crash into the lake."

Chris chuckled after saying this, but Colin didn't so much as a return a polite smile to the morbid joke. He understood the gravity of the situation and was in no laughing mood. Chris returned the syringe to the first-aid kit and snapped it shut, clapping his hands.

"That's it?" Colin asked.

"That's it. You have some sacred blood in your system now. I suggest you get this bird ready to fly and hide like I suggested. Remember, if you let out a peep about this, you'll catch a bullet to the head within twenty-four hours—you can take that to the bank, my friend. Hopefully if everything plays out the way it should, you and I can resume our normal lives."

"Isn't this blood in me forever now?"

"Of course, but I just need you to stay safe temporarily. Once I'm back on my feet, I'll work on finding a more permanent successor to help stretch my life out longer." Chris's stomach grumbled and he looked down to it with a grin. "I should get going now, and you should too."

"Yes, sir—best of luck. I hope to see you soon."

"Oh you will, and I look forward to it." Chris winked and

started for the door, waiting for Colin to open it. When he did, a gust of cold wind blew in, but it didn't bother Chris. He had too much on his mind to worry about the weather, and would be within the confines of his cabin in a few minutes.

He walked down the steps, his hunger and vulnerability the furthest things from his mind. A new confidence had grown now that he had arrived to Angle Inlet, and that was the point. He never planned to live in fear, only to live in safety until the madness passed. The Road Runners could only cover so much ground and search for so long until they gave up. Chris had a three month supply of food and water in his cabin, and wouldn't have to step foot outside for any reason.

It appeared snow had fallen a couple days earlier, patches of frozen powder scattered about the airport grounds outside of the covered hangar. The temperatures could drop into single digits, sometimes even into the negative, during the winter months, but this night was a brisk twenty degrees, good enough for the walk Chris had to endure.

He moved quickly from the hangar, passing two other jets on his way out. The cabin was deliberately built one mile south of Northwest Angle Airport. Chris had to walk the first half-mile down Inlet Road before continuing straight into the woods for the latter half. It could only be reached on foot this way, intentional to give any potential stalkers a hell of a time keeping up, let alone explain how to find the cabin. Chris always figured if his life came down to this situation, he'd be able to play the land to his advantage. He had spent the summer of 1981 living at the cabin, roaming the woods for eight hours each day to learn the area, even carving secret symbols into the trees that only made sense to him, to help navigate back to the cabin.

"Good luck catching me here, Martin Briar," Chris said as

he trudged down the road, duffel bag slung over his shoulder, hand on the pistol tucked in his waistband. His old legs cried out for help, but they'd have to wait for rest that would be plentiful once he arrived to the cabin with nothing to do but hunker down inside.

While it wasn't a vacation by any means, Chris found himself looking forward to the isolation and temporary absence from the day-to-day operations of the Revolution. He didn't worry about his organization. The Road Runners might blow up a couple more of their offices, but that would only be a distraction. All they wanted at this point in the game was Chris. He'd be surprised if they actually spent their time and energy on anything else besides catching him.

He reached the point where the road broke east toward the small town, but he kept forward, stepping into the uneven terrain of the woods. Chris stopped and unzipped the duffel bag, pulling out the flashlight and flicking it on to shine on the non-existent path ahead. The first 200 yards were easy, fairly flat and light in terms of trees. It wasn't until he hit the heavier populated trees that he'd have to locate his secret messages for guidance.

Chris continued on, unaware that back at the hangar, a Road Runner had already climbed the steps to his jet and shot Colin in the head, leaving him dead in the cockpit, face down on the control panel. That same soldier had dashed out of the jet and trailed behind Chris, following his every move, recording it on a cell phone to have the route saved for later reference.

He never heard the footsteps far behind him, his own feet crunching in the random patches of snow and echoing in the woods. Chris had no reason to look back once the road was out of sight, a costly mistake as he headed toward the cabin for a false sense of security.

Chapter 17

Martin and his team flew into Winnipeg later that night. Claudia Larsen, the Road Runner who had shot the pilot and followed Chris through the woods, had her eyes on the cabin and confirmed Chris had gone inside. She had to leave the property for a 45-minute round trip into town in order to gain better cell phone reception to place the call to Alina. Claudia tried uploading the video she had recorded of the route to the cabin from the airport, but it failed with each attempt.

Martin promised Claudia some relief, sending another soldier to meet her at precisely six in the morning to relieve her after a late night of standing in the freezing weather. He wanted to take zero risks, and planned to make his move the next night once the sun set. No one on their team had any familiarity with Angle Inlet, and they wanted to conduct some research over the course of the day to get familiar with the layout and any potential issues with carrying out this deadly mission.

The Road Runners had an office in Winnipeg, but no one dared go near it, fearful of revealing their presence to the members and causing a ruckus for the entire continent that was still under an extended blackout authorized by the Council. Alina had kept tabs on her email inbox, only reading messages, refusing to send any responses until the mission was done. After the initial four-hour blackout had passed without receiving word from Martin, the Council extended it another two hours, and repeated so all throughout the evening, and now as the clock approached midnight.

They had arrived in Canada shortly after 9 P.M. and immediately pushed all seats toward the edges of the cabin to allow more space for sleeping bags on the floor. It was crowded, but they had no other options unless they wanted to deal with checking into a hotel at the late hour.

Martin assured them that regardless of what happened, they'd all be back home in twenty-four hours, and he encouraged everyone on the jet to think about where they wanted to go on their mandatory vacation once the mission ended. The discussion lifted the spirits of everyone on the team, chatter running rampant about dream trips to Europe, the Caribbean, and Hawaii.

Martin didn't expect anyone on the jet to work throughout the night, but nearly everyone did, opening their laptops and searching the maps of Angle Inlet provided on the internet. He did the same, sipping a rum and Coke as he fought off the idea of what he'd be doing tomorrow night.

After having a feel for the many trees in the forest of Angle Inlet, Martin opened his email inbox to find over 700 unread messages, a number that was sure to exceed four digits by the time he returned to Denver and could sit behind his desk to sift through them all. Mission briefs, budget requests, and dozens of interview invitations from the media filled the top of his inbox, but one message stood out with its subject written in capital letters: RESPOND IMMEDIATELY.

His eyes followed the line to see the sender as Chief Councilman Uribe, and he clicked on it to expand the full email:

Commander Briar,

I must inquire why you and your team have cut off communication from the entire organization. I have to believe this is the work of your Lieutenant Commander, as I have already reached out to those who knew her best in Central America. They told me it was common for her to go completely off the grid while on important missions. And while I can appreciate that from a high-ranking soldier, you both need to understand that you are in leadership positions now. Our members are very much aware that you have both vanished without a word. We're starting to receive messages demanding answers, and as you may have seen, people are taking to the streets. I feel this is your fault: perhaps if our members had seen their leader, they wouldn't have felt the need to be marching all around the continent and get news coverage from every major network around the world.

Our team is working on containing and controlling these protests, but things could be done much quicker and easier with a quick message letting us know you're alright. Can you imagine if the president of the United States hadn't been heard from in two weeks? It would cause mass hysteria, and that's what we're seeing now.

It is wrong on your part to relay communication back to headquarters every day of the mission until the actual day of you kidnapping Sonya, then stop. Did you get her? Is she dead? The suspense you have left us in is mind-blowing, and not in a good way. Our organization is currently under a blackout, and it won't be lifted until you make an appearance. I urge you to reconsider your actions and make life easier for the entire membership. One day has passed, and a second will start to spread further unrest within the Road Runners. The blackout was implemented to allow us to arrest and detain those who are protesting, but if it spills into a second day, we expect matters to snowball even further out of *control.*

We see you are alive and well, thanks to your tracking device. As I write this email it appears you are in Nevada at Wealth of Time. I unfortunately have no additional resources to send to check on you, thanks to the protests, but I assume you are safe since you are traveling with the best crew available. All I can do is trust that the mission is going successfully, and will stay out of your way. I'm giving you two more days. If we don't hear from you by then, we'll be forced to lift the blackout and make preparations for a new leadership team. Some Lead Runners around the continent have already reached out to throw in their names for consideration.

I wish you well, and hope to see you soon with a dead Chris Speidel. Godspeed.

-Chief

Martin rotated his laptop and let Alina read the message. She took a minute to skim it over before letting out a soft chuckle. "I'm impressed the Council tracked down my friends in Central America so quickly. I wonder who they reached out to."

"We need to do something, Alina. They're already talking about starting a new election. This is irresponsible."

"It will be fine. This email is all a ploy to get a response from you," Alina replied, handing the laptop back. "If they were serious, do you think he'd give you two days? He knows the mission is working and is leaving you time to finish it."

"Then why bother sending this to me?"

"He just wants the response. Even if you replied with one word, it would be something he could share with the organization to prove that you're alive. That's all this is—people worried you're dead because of what happened to Strike."

"The tracking devices are open for plenty of people to see—"

"The members don't care. Strike's tracking device was ripped out of her arm and dropped in the middle of a field. Until the people hear from you directly, they'll assume anything else that suggests you're alive is just a coverup. Keep in mind, our bunch has become very paranoid since Strike. Trust is broken, and while this precise moment doesn't help, things will get better once we finish this mission. Tensions are high, but a broken Revolution will relieve all of that tension."

Martin nodded. "I don't see the harm in sending an email back. He acknowledged he knows where we are—"

Alina shook her head viciously. "You need to read between the lines. If he knows where we are and isn't sending anyone to check on us, then he's deliberately staying out of our way. You're the *Commander*—there is no valid excuse to not even take two soldiers off the streets and send them our way."

"You really do this all the time, don't you?"

Aline smirked. "Let's just say this isn't the first time I've received an email like this, and I know it won't be the last."

"So we just sit on our hands for all of tomorrow and hope things don't spin out of control?"

Alina shrugged. "How do you think wars end? I've settled a few local wars with the cartels all over Central America, and every single one is complete chaos on both sides until the final bell is rung. I know we've been taking a beating for years from these guys, but I can assure you this is all very normal. I'd actually be surprised if people were just going about their business as usual, pretending nothing is happening."

"But they don't even know we're on this mission. They *should* be going about their days as usual."

"People have an extra sense that can read scenarios, even

when they don't realize it. It consumes them, overtakes all their reason and logic—it's almost like a poison. The fact that you and I haven't been heard from in two weeks probably started as a bit of anxiety and worry for our members. But as the days passed, that stress turned into hope and speculation. 'Are they really doing it?' people ask, first in their private homes, but eventually in larger group settings. That's what feeds the rumor mill. They piece together their theories and eventually land on the right answer. The protests are just a result of the impatience everyone has waiting for the outcome of this mission."

"And you think sending a reply to Uribe will unravel all of that hope? I guess I still don't see how it's a bad thing."

"Not at all. Sending the email isn't about the members. If they *hear* from you, but still don't *see* you, it will only throw more gasoline onto the fire. I just don't want you to send an email because we are so close. We're off the grid, as far as Chris knows, and emailing will only give him an opportunity to figure out what we're up to. He could have us hacked, for all we know. Not likely, but why risk it? We're only 125 miles away from him, and less than twenty-fours until you make your move. It's best to let outside factors handle themselves. If there are any problems, they'll still be there when you get back."

"Or they won't," Martin said with a grin, suggesting that Chris's death was indeed a magic wand that could heal all matters.

Alina returned a nod. "Now you're getting it."

"You're good. I see every day why I picked the right person."

"Stop the flattery, Commander. It makes you look weak," she said with a wink, standing up from her seat. "I'm gonna grab a glass of wine and hope it puts me to sleep. You need another drink to cap off the night?"

Martin raised his glass, still half full. "I'm good, Lieutenant. Thanks anyway."

"Have a good night, and make sure to get some sleep. Tomorrow will be the longest day of your life, so brace yourself."

She walked off, stopping to chat with a few team members as she crossed the cabin toward the back bar.

Martin closed his laptop, having enough drama from the few minutes he had it open, and leaned back in his chair to finish his drink. As sleep crept closer, the weight of his destiny ballooned in his mind. When the sun rose in the morning there would be no looking back. Plans were being formed and would be put in place, Martin the only one on the continent able to execute them.

Do it for Izzy.

Chapter 18

Chris had slipped into bed wondering if his body would actually fall asleep. With his blood now swimming in Colin's body, it was possible his return to an immortal man would make a gradual comeback, but it could take a day or two.

He fell asleep around eleven o'clock and woke up in a panic at four in the morning, jumping out of bed, paranoid that someone had broken into his cabin. The door remained locked, the air still and silent. Even before his powers as the Keeper of Time, Chris had a unique sense of the world around him, feeling eyes watching him or someone hiding in the corner of a room. No such alarms went off in his head at the moment, but his gut wrenched in a way that suggested danger was lurking.

"That's the point," Chris said to his empty cabin.

It was a small space, roughly 150 square feet with a twin bed tucked along one wall, a gas stove in the opposite corner, and his stockpile of non-perishable cans of food and bottles of water in the other. The cabin had no electricity or running water, a truly simple way of life he had hoped to avoid. Outside behind the cabin were a dozen propane tanks for the stove and several bundles of firewood should he need to build a campfire.

Chris didn't actually know how to cook food. He never did it when he was married, always ate out during his early days as a Revolter, and no longer had a need for food once becoming Keeper. He understood that canned food could be eaten directly, but might taste better after being heated up. The thought of turning on the stove didn't interest him, at least not this early in the day. For breakfast he grabbed a can of green beans, popped off the lid and started drinking the juice and vegetables straight from the can.

Chris gagged at first, the flavor bitter and earthy. He needed to head into town today to place a phone call, and considered stopping by the grocery store for eggs and bread, maybe even a box of cereal. He couldn't possibly start every day like this, and hoped the injection into Colin would kick in and make this all a moot point. The bottles of water had never looked so appealing, so he grabbed one from the mountain of cases and chugged it to rid the green bean flavor from his mouth. A huge belch worked its way up from his rumbling stomach, and Chris let it out with a satisfied grin, one of his favorite bodily functions that had vanished over the years.

For the first time since waking up after the accidental nap in his Idaho office, he had finally satisfied his hunger and was ready for the morning ahead. While he dozed last night, Chris thought about how to best approach the next two weeks and decided it was in his best interest to create as much chaos as possible around the continent. The more distractions the Road Runners had to tend to, the more likely he'd remain undisturbed in his hideout. However, he still expected a fight at some point. His eyes dashed to the duffel bag he had left near the front door, temporarily worried that it had somehow walked out during the night. All the guns and ammunition he needed were in that bag, plenty to fend off an attack. He had small slots installed around the cabin walls, spaced about two feet apart, and only three inches wide. They were meant to provide just enough room for him to stick his pistol through and shoot at chest level to whoever might be outside. The cabin had only two windows with the drapes currently drawn, but he'd open those as soon as danger arrived, ready to blast any poor soul who dared approach his property.

Chris grabbed his cell phone from the stovetop, the battery at 80% thanks to having charged it during the flight to Angle Inlet. He'd head into town, make his calls, then power off the phone for two weeks until he decided it was safe to step outside and walk back to town for an update on the situation. Fortunately, he only needed to place one call to authorize what was known as Mission Lifesaver, setting in place a chain of calls to all the Revolution chapter leaders across North America. It was a mission buried in the back of the massive Revolution handbooks that were stored in each office, but the instructions were rather straightforward.

He had fallen asleep in his all-black suit, but now took it off and reached under the bed where a rotation of different outfits waited for him to choose. They were tailored to fit in with his surroundings: jeans, sweatpants, sweaters, thick hoodies, and a heavy winter jacket. If he had walked into town wearing a suit, the locals would surely question the strange old man with frosty hair. Some might even follow him back to the cabin, which would only lead to their death and an investigation by the lone sheriff who worked in Angle Inlet.

Time no longer mattered to Chris, the next two weeks set to be strictly inside the cabin with the occasional trip outside for fresh air, alone in the wilderness. Seeing that it was only 5 A.M. didn't matter, so he finished getting dressed, slipped into the winter jacket, and stepped outside into a brisk ten degrees.

His body shivered as he kicked patches of snow, glancing around the woods, the silence maddening. A breeze whistled through the trees, and Chris remembered from the summer he had spent at the cabin how the woods tended to make sounds of their own. The slightest of sounds would echo, much like a cave. When the wind howled, the echo dragged the sound out longer, sometimes mimicking a pack of hyenas.

"Hello!" Chris barked, his voice bouncing in every direction before coming back to him like a boomerang. He stared around in amazement, mouth agape with a slight grin. His one word had turned into at least thirty words by the time the echo faded away. "Too fun," he whispered.

The cold bothered him, his joints tightening as he started through the woods, following the signs he could see more clearly thanks to dawn casting a soft orange glow across the sky. The carvings were faint, obvious only to Chris. Every other tree was numbered to point him in the right direction, the cabin being zero. Odd numbers signified a path to the north toward the airport, even numbers leading south toward town. A walk in either direction was roughly twenty minutes from the cabin, depending on the conditions. Last night had taken much longer from the airport thanks to the darkness of night.

Chris rounded the cabin and started south, the air biting his lungs with each breath. "Gonna be a long trip," he muttered under his breath, wondering why it was taking so long for his abilities to return. Alaska had been an easy choice for his previous headquarters because he had been immune to the cold weather, never having to worry about stepping outside with a jacket regardless of the temperature.

It's just two weeks, he thought. *Two weeks until getting back into the swing of things, having a full return of my abilities, and squashing the Road Runners like the miserable bugs they are.*

He giggled at the thought, shaking his head in disbelief that he had actually fallen this far, still not able to quite grasp the reality of it all. The Road Runners were supposed to be long gone by now, and he wondered where he had gone wrong. Strike's death created the divide he needed within their horrendous organization, but he never could land the final blow. Their structure had too many checks and balances in place, the failed mission of killing all their Council perhaps the critical turning point. If that had been accomplished as planned, they would have had no one to turn to, no rulebook to check and see who must take power. Anarchy would have swept through the Road Runners, leaving every single member vulnerable without the protection of the organization behind them.

"Keep moving," he told himself, pushing through the only uphill portion of the route. "You can still make it happen, just make the phone call."

Chris pulled his phone out of his pocket, just to see if it had caught any signal. It hadn't, and he hobbled faster through the never-ending stand of trees, ignoring the sharp pains that gnawed on his leg.

After gaining another hundred feet on the ground, he froze and spun around, convinced he heard footsteps behind him. At least forty tall, lanky trees stared back, the soft echo of his own footsteps still bouncing around. He stood there for an entire minute, scanning left to right and back again. "Hello?" he called out, not for fun this time, but because his paranoia was getting the best of him. He didn't feel eyes watching him, but he did sense a presence in the area.

His voice ricocheted around the trees like a pinball, and when it died down, left him back in the deafening silence.

Gain your composure, man, he told himself. *No one knows you're here, and even if they did, they'd have no way of finding you. That's the point—always has been for this little shack in the woods.*

Chris nodded before pivoting back around and continuing toward the town. "Don't lose your mind," he whispered to himself, weary of having his voice continue to swirl around him as he trudged through the trees. "This is *not* the time."

The sounds of footsteps continued, but he brushed them aside as his own echoes. He stole a glance over his shoulders every few steps, but never saw anyone. Once his invincibility kicked back in, he'd have nothing to fear and could go for a simple stroll through the woods without worry. "What's taking so long?"

He started to wonder if something had indeed happened to Colin. The plane could have actually crashed into the surrounding lakes and no one would ever know. And until Chris felt a sense of normalcy, he had to assume his life was still in danger. The trip to town needed to be quick, as any additional time spent away from the cabin increased the chances of the situation spiraling out of control. But the call needed to be placed, plus an attempt to hear from Colin and know that he was okay.

Twenty minutes passed and he finally reached the edge of the trees where a lone three-block road, Main Street, stretched with every store and service available in town. At such an early hour, only the coffee shop appeared to have its lights on, a half-dozen people inside enjoying their boost to start the day. Chris remembered that simplicity of life, having done the same thing each morning before heading to the factories, getting familiar with those same faces across the shop, a sense of community.

He shook the nostalgia and checked his cell phone, the beautiful sight of service bars greeting him, and dialed the head of their Chicago chapter, a younger gentleman by the name of Patrick Williams.

"Pat! How are you, my good sir?" Chris greeted once he answered.

"Chris?!" Patrick replied, his voice deep, but clearly surprised. "Where the hell are you? People are starting to talk."

"Yes, I know. Pat, we have entered Mission Lifesaver. Start the process and get word out to all of our lovely Revolters that this mission is currently active. They know what to do."

"Holy shit, sir, so it's true. No one ever thought this would happen."

Thanks for rubbing it in, Chris thought. "Thank you, Pat, neither did I, but we must focus and get out of this. I'm not going to worry, and neither should anyone else. This plan is tailored to get things back to normal. Now get the ball rolling."

"Yes, sir. Take care of yourself."

Patrick hung up and the wheels of madness were officially in motion. Within three hours, most of the major cities in North America would burn to the ground in a coordinated effort that would leave national governments scrambling, the Road Runners unable to do anything but run, all while the Revolution sat back and watched, laughing.

Chris wasted no time dialing Colin, keeping his head up to watch for anyone who might spot him from Main Street. No one did, but the phone rang and rang until eventually dropping the call. He tried one more time, getting the same result, and stuffing the phone back into his pocket as he swirled around and started back into the woods. "Dammit!" he snarled, stomping on the snow, kicking any of the heavy sticks that dared get in his path.

All Chris wanted was some assurance that his life wasn't in danger. His rage boiled up to the point he no longer felt the fatigue in his old legs. He considered sprinting for his cabin, but didn't trust his body to handle such a task, especially under his hot head.

A trip to the grocery store had to wait now—it was time to hunker down until matters sorted themselves out.

Chapter 19

Mission Lifesaver was designed to do quite the opposite of its title. The only life it meant to save was that of Chris Speidel, never mind the potential thousands of casualties that were sure to fall once the mission was complete.

No one in the Road Runners knew about this mission by the Revolution, thanks to it being one of its best kept secrets. For those Road Runner soldiers on the streets, trying to contain the mass protests that now carried on every minute of the day, word had arrived that the Wealth of Time store in Nevada no longer existed. This news spread among both the soldiers and those protesting, prompting raucous celebration by those who understood this to be the first step toward the collapse of the Revolution. It fueled their fire, making them believe their international protests had somehow led to this happening, forever oblivious that Commander Briar was going to move forward with this mission regardless of what any of the membership felt.

As they tended to be, the Road Runners were organized to a fault, even during mass, public unrest. They had numbers and they knew it, setting up shifts for different groups of protesters to show up and relieve the group before them. It had become an around-the-clock phenomenon with no end in sight. They remained disciplined, not peeping a word to the local media, not chanting anything that might give away their grand secret. It was the ultimate display of unity, millions of people across North America protesting in the streets, and not an ounce of correct speculation from those in the regular world following the story.

Since they had the luxury of different shifts, everyone could check the news channels and internet to see what the world thought of their display. Rumors swirled, claiming the people were part of a Satanic cult sent to the United States for a show-down against Christianity. Others speculated it was the actual New World Order, causing a distraction while they furthered some sort of underground agenda. It was all gibberish and baseless.

No one had any intent to invoke violence during the protests. They understood the organization had issued a blackout, cutting off the power to all official offices, demanding people stay home or otherwise face punishment. But the soldiers had no way of enforcing these measures, especially now that local police had arrived and the Road Runners couldn't exactly start arresting people in front of them. The protest hadn't been planned, so no credit was due, but things definitely worked out in their favor, leaving the protesters at an impasse with the Road Runner soldiers and free to continue their cause.

By the time the news broke of the Nevada store, plans formulated to drag out the protests until word was received that Chris Speidel had been killed. Then it would turn into a mass party. Until then, they had to hold their ground and keep focused.

In Denver, the gathering had swelled to just over six thousand people at Civic Center Park, right across the street from the state capitol. Several Road Runners made the trip to Denver, sensing something magnificent on the horizon, wanting to be in the city of their new headquarters for whatever might ensue.

One Road Runner in particular, Kelly Winters, made the trip down from Casper, Wyoming, where she lived alone, enjoying life as a Road Runner in a cozy cottage where she spent the days painting pictures, writing books and poems, and cooking challenging meals every night.

She had heard about the protests well before the blackout was issued, and was already on her way, not willing to turn back. Kelly wanted to be part of the movement that would lead to the Revolution's downfall, and understood that any gathering of Road Runners would come with little to no risk of personal harm. She had seen the initial march down Sixteenth Street Mall on the Road Runners' network, and that's what prompted her to pack an overnight bag and get in the car.

Kelly arrived downtown at eight in the morning, after having spent the night at a hotel, unsure where exactly to go or who to meet up with. She simply found the crowd and joined in, her thin frame and short height not ideal for pushing her way through a crowd of thousands. Helicopters circled above, Denver police manned the perimeter, and a group of four Road Runners stood on the stage of the park's small amphitheater, speaking into a megaphone that echoed across the way.

The closer she got, the sturdier the wall of Road Runners became, making her move down the line to seek any soft spots that would allow her to inch closer to the stage. She didn't drive all this way to stand in the back and not hear anything, let alone have no idea who was speaking. A woman's voice carried from the front. "We've been here for two days now, and we think change is finally on its way. We must remain strong in this fight and demand the outcome we want to see. We have what it takes to stay here for much longer. The longer we fight, the harder it becomes for them to deny our needs."

People applauded at different moments, but everyone was engaged, heads glued to the stage, nodding, minds open to the new day's wave of confidence. It uplifted Kelly, being part of something so much bigger than herself, and she focused on the speaker, a middle-aged woman with short gray hair and a pair of glasses that kept needing to be pushed up as her head bobbed from speaking with such conviction.

Kelly stood on her tiptoes, now 100 yards away from the stage where she found the perfect gap between two people's shoulders for a clear view.

The speaker paced back and forth, dropping her head as she spoke into the megaphone, and held up a free hand, index finger pointing high. "Something special is coming. It's been a long two days, but we have to remain patient. When the news comes that we've been waiting for our entire lives, don't be afraid to bask in its glory. Hug the person next to you. Jump for joy. Scream to the heavens above. Because when we win, we'll know that we all played a part in making it happen."

The crowd howled in deafening unison. A sound of fireworks exploded from the back. Kelly looked up to the sky to see, but none ever appeared. It was possible the sun was too bright for a clear view of fireworks, but they kept going off, nearly drowned out by the applause and hollering of those around her.

"RUN!" a frantic voice shouted from somewhere in the sea of people. Kelly spun around, but couldn't see anything besides other faces staring ahead, a few others also looking toward the back.

The rapid explosions continued with no fireworks to complement them, and after another thirty seconds passed, a dozen people started charging toward the stage, barreling through the crowd, shoving people aside, blood oozing from their faces and limbs. They never looked back, keeping their heads forward, running for their lives.

Kelly whipped back around to the stage. The group that had been up there watched with dazed confusion before flinging the megaphone aside and sprinting in the opposite direction.

The crowd followed their gaze and reaction, bolting into action. Kelly remained frozen in place, hoping that people were overreacting, partly curious what had unfolded in the back of the audience. As the space cleared within moments, she caught a glimpse of a new wall of people running, mouths hanging open, fear brushed over their faces. The explosions continued, a handful of runners falling dead to the ground.

It wasn't until this moment she realized the fireworks were not fireworks at all, but the constant chorus of gunfire. Her heart raced as this reality settled in, her thoughts scattering as she processed the fact that had she given up and stayed toward the back of the crowd, she would likely be one of the dozens of bodies lying face down.

A row of black vans barricaded the north side of the park, the easiest route to leave. Side doors swung open, stationary machine guns showering bullets in every direction.

The police had opened fire on the vans, but they were simply outnumbered, several blue uniforms splayed into the mix of death all around the park grounds. "LONG LIVE THE REVOLUTION!" screamed a masked man in the van, waving both of his middle fingers to the crowd that had dispersed.

Fires had been set in the trash cans, and Kelly saw a huddle of people lighting Molotov cocktails, tossing them onto the corpses. Across the street, beneath the glimmering golden dome of the capitol, more people dressed in all black had raided the property, deadly cocktails sailing toward the building and breaking through the glass.

The adrenaline had finally reached its peak, forcing Kelly to look away from the madness and sprint, guns still firing away with no mercy, no rest. The park had become a maze of death, dodging bullets and dead bodies as she fled for safety behind the amphitheater. She tripped on someone's lifeless limbs, tumbling for a moment and rolling onto another dead body, before jumping to her feet and scampering once more.

A burning sensation struck her left calf, like someone had pressed a hot iron directly to her flesh, but not even that forced her back to the ground. She limped, taking long strides with her good leg, dragging her bad one behind as blood left a scattered trail behind it. A small crowd had formed behind the amphitheater, but the majority of protesters sprinted away from the park, some three blocks away already with no sign of slowing down.

Kelly leaned against the concrete wall, panting for breath, head spinning in every direction as she half-expected someone to walk up and shoot her right in the face. That didn't happen, but something much worse was already unfolding across the street.

The timing didn't make sense, then again, she had no way of clearly judging time once the chaos had erupted. Ten seconds felt like twenty minutes.

The capitol's dome had caught fire, smaller patches of flames spreading across the rest of the exterior as more and more explosives were thrust against the building. Traffic came to a halt on Broadway as mobs of the black-cloaked Revolters swarmed the streets and sidewalks, their numbers trying to match those of the protesters who were assembled just minutes ago.

Not all Road Runners had fled the scene, however, and some engaged in combat, swinging desperate punches, shooting from behind trees. A few Revolters took a beating, some dying next to their own victims, but the remaining Road Runners were no match.

Kelly let her body slide down the wall until she sat on the ground, her blasted leg turning completely numb as blood pooled, running in a small stream toward the bloody footprints scattered across the ground. She fainted, unaware that similar attacks were unfolding all around the continent, the Revolution throwing everything they had as they, too, sensed the major event set to occur in the time travel world.

Chapter 20

The early morning had passed rather uneventfully for Martin and the team on the jet. Two members had wandered into downtown Winnipeg to buy three dozen doughnuts for a simple breakfast to feed everyone.

Before the food arrived, Martin went into the bathroom and vomited into the toilet. He only had consumed one drink the night before, but his stomach flipped cartwheels all night as he speculated on the possibility that his life might end today. And if not his, then that of Chris, which was as equally stressful of a thought. As much as he had wanted a deep sleep, it never came. He woke nearly every hour, staring at the ceiling, reflecting on his life, trying to make sense of how and why it all led to this point. Speculation remained that he had somehow been planted in this role since the beginning, but he had concluded there were too many moving parts to make it all happen, accepting his destiny to remove the madman from the world.

His arms trembled, legs hollow and weak when he stood from the recliner to begin the day. He was the first one up at five o'clock, most of the team sound asleep, some faintly stirring, as they had collapsed straight into their laptops at some point in the night.

After he puked, Martin returned to the recliner to relax. He glanced around the jet cabin, admiring such a phenomenal team who had given their all, pushing themselves to the brink for the greater good. The Road Runners would have found a way to defeat Chris without him—their talent and dedication ran too deep.

People gradually woke up as the morning grew later, Alina among one of the first. Her hair stood in a frazzled mess as she stepped around the sleeping bodies on the floor, offering a polite, but embarrassed, grin to Martin as she made her way to the bathroom. She didn't say a word, and neither did he.

The jet had two bathrooms, one in the front, one in the rear, and Martin watched as lines formed at both, glad he had been able to beat the rush. He worried about making it all the way to nightfall, his brain already having the slightest itch of fatigue. The day would surely be engaging enough to distract from his urge to sleep. He didn't know if commanders ever took time off, but if things played out the way they hoped, he might become the first one to start a new tradition. It had to have been at least two years since he last had a full eight hours of sleep in a single night, but he had grown to live with the exhaustion, sometimes thriving in the state of mind that bordered on delirium.

None of that matters today, Martin thought. *Throw the play-book out the window. You'll be on Chris's turf. Man against a withering old man for all the glory, alone in a frozen world until someone goes home and the other lays dead on the ground.*

The thoughts brought a return of the twisting inside. He thought he might vomit again, but there was nothing left.

Alina returned from the bathroom, dressed in athletic pants and a long-sleeved t-shirt. Most everyone on the jet dressed the same way, all of their clothes originally packed from the two-week stay in Chicago. Martin was the only one stepping outside of the jet—him plus whoever was driving him to Angle Inlet. It had been decided he would drive to his destination rather than fly into the local airport. The Revolution's private jet was already parked in the two-plane hangar and was surely grabbing attention from the locals. Having a second jet of equal elegance would surely prompt a full-blown investigation by the ninety residents who called the small peninsula home.

The main objective for the day was to remain off the radar. Flying literally showed up on radars, and crossing an international border was something they'd rather not deal with after making it to Winnipeg with no commotion from Canadian officials. Driving wasn't ideal, but a two-hour trip was just reasonable enough to make a case for the method of transportation. Arielle Lucila was the main candidate to drive the commander, but had yet to be formally confirmed.

By nine o'clock, the entire team had woken and the jet hummed with energy and excited chatter. Some continued right back to work, preparing final research before the big presentation was due to be delivered to Martin at 12:30, part of his final preparation before leaving. Others gathered around, chomping on doughnuts, slamming back enough coffee to ride out the rest of the day. Martin made his rounds, partaking in small talk with his team to help keep his mind off the clock and the inevitable task that stood at the end of the road.

The next two hours passed in a blur until time came to a screeching halt shortly after eleven o'clock. "Holy shit!" Arielle shouted. "The capitol in Denver is on fire, and there are reports of hundreds dead at the protests."

Dozens of hands reached into pockets to retrieve cell phones, wanting to see the story for themselves.

"It's happening everywhere," Arielle continued. "The national news outlets aren't even sure which one to cover. It has to be the Revolution—all the attacks have been carried out on the 'unknown protesters who have caused a stir the last couple of days.'"

"Settle down, everyone," Alina barked, moving to the center of the room. "Let's not jump to conclusions—especially not today. It probably is the Revolution, but let's make sure. I want everyone to get online and check the local news from whatever city you were born. See what you can find."

The jet fell silent as everyone brushed anxious thumbs over their cell phones, skimming the news, checking Twitter feeds, all to find out a bigger picture of the incidents.

"Same thing in St. Louis!" someone shouted.

"Mexico City."

"Philadelphia."

"Toronto."

"Milwaukee."

The list of cities continued until more than twenty different locations had been called out. Martin joined Alina in the middle of the room. "This is a coordinated effort across the continent. Are there reports of anything like this happening outside of North America?"

Everyone looked around to each other, but no one responded.

"That proves it. We expected as much, though I'll admit, not something as ferocious as these early reports suggest. They took advantage of all the Road Runners huddled together at those protests and killed as many as they could."

Some of the team members began crying, eyes glued to their phones as they read the stories breaking from all around North America, Martin's words falling on distraught ears.

"This is meant to distract us," Alina said. "Don't let it

happen. We can see the finish line and we *must* keep our eyes on it. We have one more hour until delivering our remarks to Commander Briar—I suggest you work on that. There will be plenty of time afterwards to shift our focus to these attacks, but for now we *must* remain on schedule. So let's take a moment, gather our thoughts, and get back to finishing what we started over two weeks ago."

Alina turned and grabbed Martin by the arm, pulling him back to their two seats along the wall. "I know what you're thinking, but we cannot reach out to the Council."

"Of course we can," Martin snapped. "We have to."

"And tell them what? Half of those dead bodies are our own soldiers. We're at the mercy of the Revolution and can only hope the local police officers have a chance. Hopefully some of the National Guard is still around—they'll have the best odds."

Martin shook his head. "I can't believe this is really happening. Of all the days."

Alina shrugged. "I get it, this is awful, but we have to look at the big picture. This is a compliment to what we've been able to achieve. I guarantee you this all started once Chris realized something was wrong with Sonya. We don't know what he found out before fleeing, but it's clear something sparked a panic. Their entire organization sees the writing on the wall, and this is their desperate attempt to stop it from happening."

"Am I going to meet an army when I get to his cabin?"

"Doesn't matter—they'll be frozen."

"What if he found another Warm Soul, and has them waiting for me? I'd have no chance."

"Commander, with all due respect, you're letting your thoughts get the best of you. We've done our research and have kept tabs on the known Warm Souls around the entire world.

143

None of them have moved, or even been contacted by Chris, from what we can tell. You'll have the one-on-one situation that we've been planning for all along."

Martin took a deep breath, the rest of the jet falling into background noise as he tried to process the unfolding chaos. "Thank you, Lieutenant. Please don't think it's a matter of trust—I know how hard everyone has been working to make this mission as seamless as possible. I had a long night and have thought over every single detail of how things will play out later. Naturally, I can only imagine the worst-case scenario for everything: the car crashes on the way, we get stopped at the border by Revolters, Steffan goes missing right before we need to freeze time. All of that ran through my head, and still is."

Alina nodded. "I completely understand. I used to do the same thing, Commander. But I've come to understand that the more preparation that goes into a mission, the odds of something going wrong fall drastically. And if I may, I've never seen a mission as thoroughly planned out as this. For God's sake, we have alternate routes for your drive, and there *are* no alternate routes. Think about that. Most missions have five to seven people working on them, and this one has twenty-four. The prep work was so spread across the board and cross-checked that not a single detail has gone unnoticed. You will be delivered safely to that cabin with only one worry to concern yourself with. Do you understand?"

Martin pursed his lips, nodding, rummaging his thoughts for a counterargument, or at least an excuse. But he had nothing, silenced by his number two to trust the process. After his big speech giving all the credit to this once-in-a-lifetime team, Martin had been the last person to listen to his own words. Now that he did, he felt somewhat better, although nothing could erase the worry of death that lingered above him like a black cloud. Everyone else on the jet was in a light mood, at least before the news had broken of the Revolution's attacks. They didn't have to worry about waking up tomorrow; Martin did.

"Thank you, Lieutenant. Let's get to work."

Chapter 21

Despite the morning's commotion, plans continued on time for the Road Runners stuck on the jet. Half past noon arrived and Alina called attention to the team, standing in front of the wall that separated the cabin from the cockpit.

"I hope everyone has taken a moment to gather themselves. I know we are all worried about our loved ones back wherever you might call home. We're helpless on this jet, and I know the first thing I'll be doing is flying to Central America to make sure my friends and family are okay. I suggest you avoid the news for the remainder of the afternoon. If you don't, you're only going to drive yourself mad. That is all I'm going to say regarding this matter, and I'll be happy to revisit it once we hear the good news from Commander Briar later tonight.

"As you know, we set this time aside for a final briefing on what Commander Briar is to expect. I know this presented a unique challenge for us as a team, as every mission we've ever worked on has dealt with multiple Road Runners and how to best position our team for success. This mission, once the commander is dropped off in Angle Inlet, will be just him. While it might sound easier to plan, on the surface, I know it was much harder than we are used to. So thank you for your dedication, especially for having to do most of this work on the fly. Give yourselves a round of applause." A few scattered hands clapped, but the energy had shifted to a much darker mood since Martin's speech last night. "Arielle, will you please join me up here?"

Heads turned as they followed Arielle making her way from the middle of the jet to the front, greeting Alina with a warm smile.

"I've reviewed all of the research and will present it for us all to see," Alina continued. "Should something sound incorrect, please notify us immediately—do not be afraid to interrupt."

She nodded toward the back of the room where a man flicked on a projector, its image blasting across the front wall and prompting Alina and Arielle to step aside. Martin remained near his seat, but had a clear view of the presentation.

A map of Canada filled the screen, a heavy purple line running from Winnipeg to Angle Inlet, three thinner lines branching off in different directions, but still arriving to the same destination.

"Arielle will drive Commander Briar. All research has been completed on this route, and we've found it to be rather straightforward. There is one construction zone that spans two-miles, but it's in the middle of nowhere, so we don't anticipate much of a slowdown from it. We confirmed Winnipeg has been attacked by the Revolution, and the Canadian army has been deployed to control the situation. It doesn't appear this will affect the car's departure, but the situation is changing by the minute, so something to be aware of. Even if that changes, we highly doubt it will affect our ability to *leave* Winnipeg. A military-grade SUV has been ordered and will arrive here to the jet at five o'clock tonight. Arielle and Commander Briar will be leaving at 5:30 sharp. We project the drive will take two hours and eighteen minutes. Another car will arrive in fifteen minutes from now, in which we have four of our members driving the route and coming right back to report the most up-to-date information. Felix, Megan, Selena, Lucas—are you all ready?"

The four were gathered in the back and gave a thumbs up.

"Perfect. They will report to us in real time from the road anything they see out of the ordinary. If everything comes back as normal, Arielle and the commander will leave on time with no worries. She will drive him into downtown Angle Inlet where Commander Briar will walk through the woods—it is the only way to reach Chris's cabin."

The screen changed, zooming into Angle Inlet and showing a dotted path from Main Street to the middle of the woods.

"Commander Briar will have a printout of this exact map. It's a rather simple path, hard to get lost, as we've counted it out by the step for where to turn. Commander Briar, have you reviewed this information yet?"

"Yes, ma'am," Martin replied, holding up the laminated copy of the map. "Planned to the very last branch on every tree," he said with a chuckle.

"The terrain is tricky and we've obtained a special pair of hiking boots made for both a rough walk and the cold weather. The forecast calls for the temperature to be sixteen degrees Fahrenheit by the time Commander Briar starts his journey into the woods. Thank you to the team who made the venture out last night to grab supplies. We also grabbed a new winter coat, gloves, handwarmers, and beanies for Commander Briar to choose from. He will not be left in the cold should he happen to get lost in the woods."

The screen changed to show an hourly breakdown of the evening, starting at 5:30 when Martin was expected to leave.

"Commander Briar will call Steffan Privvy when he steps out of the car in Angle Inlet—we project that time will be 7:48, give or take five minutes. We have confirmed Steffan is ready and will be in isolation free of distraction at that time. It will be 1:48 in the morning in England. Time will be frozen for exactly ninety minutes after the phone call. This allows more than an hour for Commander Briar at the cabin—the walk is expected to take twenty minutes. All of the plans we have made lead us up to this point. We don't know what will happen while time is frozen, nor will we realize that time is frozen. While the world stops for us, Commander Briar will hunt down Chris Speidel and carry out an execution. He will be equipped with a light duffel bag containing a first-aid kit, two handguns, one hunting knife, one pack of matches, and one box of ammunition.

"Arielle will remain downtown and park at a discreet location. When time is unfrozen, she will follow the same path to the cabin to ensure that Commander Briar is okay. She has been instructed to keep a low profile, ducking behind trees, in case Chris manages to survive. Commander Briar has also been instructed to kill anyone else he encounters while time is frozen, leaving no threat to Arielle outside of Chris.

"We have a second team departing the jet at six o'clock. They will serve as a cleanup crew for the conclusion of this mission. Darius and Marie have volunteered to drive a van to Angle Inlet with hopes of bringing Chris's body back. Between them, Commander Briar, and Arielle, we will have a team of four able to carry the dead body through the woods. One key point we want to emphasize is that Chris should not be left alone, even as a corpse. Under no circumstance should everyone abandon the body—one person must always stay beside it.

"After that point, the body will be loaded and returned here."

"Why wouldn't we just fly to Angle Inlet to meet everyone?" a voice asked from the back of the room.

"Good question, but it plays into not causing a scene, especially when we'll have a dead body to load onto the jet."

The fact there would likely be a corpse sent a chill down Martin's back. Alina hadn't clarified *whose* dead body, just acknowledged that there would be one.

"Now, we want to hold off on making any announcements right away. There are plans surrounding what will happen to the body once we have it, and those are details I'd rather not get into now. With the major cities currently burning, we want to make sure those matters are under something that resembles control before announcing what has happened. I still want everyone to stay out of contact with anyone outside of this team until I instruct otherwise. We don't know how the Road Runners or Revolution will react to the news, and want to make sure that we'll be within the safety of our jet. Commander Briar will deliver a speech, and that will be the end of this mission. Are there any questions?"

Alina spoke in such a nonchalant manner that one might wonder if the mission was a simple grocery run, not their lifelong, wildest dream. Martin, who normally had a list of questions before jumping into a situation, found himself with nothing to ask. All bases had been covered and he knew exactly where he needed to be, and where the rest of his team would be.

No one asked additional questions, the weight off their shoulders, the reality of a finish line both daunting and exciting. Alina stood at the front with Arielle for an entire minute in awkward silence, making sure no one had anything to add.

"Alright then, thank you again for your work on this mission.

Our first car should be here any second for our team to drive the route. It's going to be a long afternoon and evening while we wait. We will make dinner arrangements for the team, but in the meantime, I only ask that we leave Commander Briar alone as he prepares for his night ahead. Our thoughts are with you, Commander, and I want to take this moment to thank you for taking this on and risking it all. I know, as do you, that this team has driven this mission, but it will be you who is forever enshrined as the hero who killed Chris. And don't you ever forget that."

Tears welled in Alina's eyes as she delivered her closing remarks, and the team erupted into applause, clapping and whistling in Martin's direction. He clasped his hands in front of his chest and bowed toward his team, never having felt so smothered in admiration. Every person on this jet would lay down their life for him—he knew that without a doubt. But tonight wasn't about that. It was his turn to put his life on the line.

No one else could.

Chapter 22

Martin leaned back in his recliner, the team dispersing away as they respected Alina's call to give him space in these moments before hitting the road. His flask of Juice throbbed in his pocket, and as much as he knew he shouldn't take a quick trip into the past, the temptation was simply too much for him as he stared death in the eyes.

There had been plenty of instances where he didn't get the closure he needed from those closest to him, but only one mattered that he'd risk slipping away for a few moments. Part of his late night tossing and turning was spent on thinking of the best way to slip in and out of the past without being caught.

I'm the Commander and don't have to explain myself to anyone on this jet, he thought. But he looked around and knew that wasn't true. It was wrong, perhaps unethical, to disappear moments before finishing the most crucial mission that ever existed. He knew his mind shouldn't have even been distracted with anything else besides the mission, but the thought of potential death—combined with the unique, tempting access to time travel—left too many doors open.

Despite all of the preparation that had gone into the mission, Martin considered his odds of survival a fifty-fifty coin toss. Alina had confirmed as much when she admitted no one knew exactly how the scene would unfold once Martin arrived to Chris's cabin. It could end within two seconds, leaving Martin dead in the snow.

I came into this time travel world for one thing, and I'm not leaving without at least saying goodbye the proper way.

He patted his pocket to confirm his wallet was there, then stood and crossed the jet to the bathroom, a couple of team members shuffling out of the way to clear a path in the cramped space. Martin kept his head down, avoiding conversation, making it seem like he was in a rush to get in the bathroom.

He promptly locked the door behind him, testing to ensure no one could get in. He debated playing a video or music, but the jet was already plenty loud thanks to the constant chatter. Ten minutes is all that would pass, and he supposed any amount of time longer in the bathroom might cause some people to worry and check on him.

Stop wasting time and get out of here.

Martin pulled out his flask and wallet, flipping it open to the small portrait of Izzy he had carried since she was alive. It had definitely aged, its white border yellowing, the edges somewhat tattered despite being inside the flimsy protective sleeve. Freckles of lint and dust splattered across the surface, but nothing could take away from Izzy's glowing smile and cheerful, bright eyes from her sixth grade school photo.

He shook his head, thinking of all the life that had occurred since her disappearance. All of the dark, gloomy days with no end in sight. From his world being flipped upside down when he had met Chris—and when he actually had his hopes up—to everything that had unfolded since then, seemed a blur.

He dropped to the floor and curled into a fetal position, not having any other options for his body to lay safely while it went to sleep for the next ten minutes. He unscrewed the flask, keeping the photo tight in his grip, and sipped, thinking specifically of February 12th, 1995 at four o'clock in the morning.

Martin screwed the lid back on, stuffed the flask into his pocket and let himself drift away, the faint rumbling visible only to him as the current world in 2020 gave way to twenty-five years earlier.

* * *

He woke up on the ground in the blistering cold of Winnipeg, jumping to his feet in a panic. He shouldn't have expected anything different, but the weather still caught him by surprise after being stuck on the jet for the last two days. He chose 4 A.M. with hopes of catching the next flight south. Being at an airport hangar already was convenient, and he made his way across the tarmac toward the terminal. All the glitz and glamour that had surrounded the airport in 2020 were gone: the hotels, shops, dozens of car rental offices. He saw one hotel, no stores, and only three car rental offices. The rest of the space was open fields or runways.

The terminal was roughly 500 yards away, so Martin broke into a run. The freezing air attacked his lungs, feeling like tiny icicles poking him with each breath he took. The grounds were dark, still pitch-black as the sun wouldn't rise for another couple hours, but that was fine with Martin as he moved in the shadows.

He reached the terminal and entered three minutes later,

having slowed toward the end of his long run, huffing and puffing as the building's warmth coated his shivering body. He took a moment to gather himself before heading for the ticket counter.

A tall, slender woman greeted him, reminding Martin of Sonya at first glance, thanks to her flowing blonde hair and big, blue eyes. "*Bonjour*, how can I help you?" she asked with a slight French accent.

"Good morning," Martin said, still catching his breath. "I'm looking for a flight to Denver, Colorado. Do you have anything direct?"

"One moment, please," she said, pursing her lips and looking down to the bulky mid-90's computer. The basic technology brought a grin to Martin's lips as nostalgia swept over him, forever appreciative for having lived through it. "Looks like we have a direct flight that leaves at ten, and one with a connection in Salt Lake City leaving at 8:45."

Martin closed his eyes and did the rough math. "I'm afraid those won't work. I'm trying to be in downtown Denver by noon Mountain Time. Do you by chance have any private charters I can take?"

She looked him up and down, clearly judging the raggedy outfit he had worn to lounge around his own private jet. "Sir, a private flight will cost at least 10,000 American dollars."

"Perfect. Do you have one available?"

She frowned and returned her attention to the computer. "I can have one ready to leave here in 90 minutes."

"I'll take it." Martin whipped his wallet back out and slapped his credit card on the counter, hoping it would scan in their machine. She stared like it was a foreign object, then shrugged before grabbing it and swiping it through the card scanner.

"Thank you, Mr. Briar," she said, passing over a receipt for his signature. "Are you traveling alone?"

"Yes. Just me, no luggage. I've had an emergency and need to get to Denver as quickly as possible." Martin felt the need to explain his situation because of his current appearance and odd request at such an early hour.

"Certainly. We don't normally bring private charters to the terminal, but since it is early in the day and our commercial flights don't start until after six, I've arranged for you to board the charter at gate twelve."

"I appreciate that. You've been a great help. What is your name?"

"Christine, but my friends call me Chris."

"I'm sure they do," Martin said with a grin. *Good one, universe,* he thought before grabbing his ticket and heading for his gate. The terminal was abandoned, only a coffee stand open, so Martin stopped for a drink and pastry. His nerves had actually settled now that he was roaming 1995, his impending duel with Chris the furthest thing from his mind.

Once he grabbed one of the several open seats at his gate, Martin realized it wasn't 1995 that had brought him joy, but being away from the bustle of the Road Runners and the commandership. With the organization in a blackout, and his team physically with his body on the jet, no one had eyes on him. He could live an entire life in a different era and avoid the showdown in ten-minute increments at a time. He even considered taking one of these farewell tours to get the closure with everyone he had lost in the past few years.

Mom and Sonya.

The temptation was certainly strong, but he'd resist. Pushing his worries off only prolonged the subconscious stress that he had so far managed to ignore. Also, no one on his team would believe that he had to spend ten minutes in the bathroom on three different occasions during the afternoon. Questions would come, as would the knocking on the door, and eventually someone breaking it down and catching him asleep on the floor, knowing damn well what he was up to.

That scene would certainly throw all their plans out the window, sparking a chaotic event where everyone on board jumped around time to find their commander who had wandered off on his own.

"Just Izzy," he muttered, stuffing a bite of lemon cake into his mouth. *Just gotta see Izzy one final time and never look back again.*

Chapter 23

The rest of the wait and flight went smoothly for Martin. Much to his delight, he managed to fall asleep naturally during the trip. He had met the pilots when boarding the jet, an older gentleman by the name of Albert Fournier who had flown fighter jets for the Canadian Air Force during the tail end of World War II, and another man around Martin's age who didn't care to share his name or past, instead focusing on his work in the cockpit while Albert shared small-talk with Martin.

Once they took off, Martin drifted away, his cares gradually leaving his brain, the pressures of his role vanishing as he flew miles above the Earth, alone, not a soul concerned with his whereabouts.

The flight took four hours and he woke just in time to see downtown Denver in the distance as they landed at Stapleton International Airport a few minutes away. Martin had forgotten that the new and improved Denver International had not been opened yet, and this shaved at least forty-five minutes off from his plans, leaving him even more time to kill.

He wished Albert farewell and thanked him for the flight before disembarking the jet and wandering through a terminal he never imagined he'd see again. The airport flooded his senses with nostalgia, remembering the few trips he and Lela had taken before Izzy was born, and the couple they had taken with her as a child.

He arrived in Denver at nine in the morning, and his plans to see Izzy weren't until noon. The airport bustled with people taking business trips, as he noticed several suits and blazers around the concourse. Martin pushed through the crowds, grateful to have no luggage, and made his way outside where a taxi stand stood, the attendant a short, dark-skinned man running back and forth from his podium to various taxis as he opened the doors for his customers.

Martin stood in line for only five minutes, smiling when he stepped up for his turn.

"Good morning, sir. Where are you headed?" the man asked, Martin catching his name as Jamal from the name tag clipped to his shirt.

"Sixteenth Street Mall, downtown," Martin said.

"Come this way."

Jamal bolted away, passing four other taxis until opening a door toward the end of the line. Martin struggled to keep up, but Jamal waited with the same, wide smile on his face before slamming the door and banging the top of the vehicle as it pulled away.

"Good morning," the cab driver said over his shoulder. "Headed downtown, right?"

"Yes, sir."

"We just missed the morning rush hour—should be ten minutes until we get there. Anywhere in particular on the mall you need to be dropped at?"

"Sixteenth and Welton would be good, and I'll take it from there."

"You got it, chief."

The cab sped away and weaved through cars, not making an effort to the driver's liking. Martin hung on for his life in the backseat, clinging to the handle above the door to not slide around like a loose bag of groceries.

The driver didn't say another word until they arrived, letting Martin know he owed eight dollars. Martin stepped out of the car and basked in the energy of downtown Denver. He stood at the exact intersection he had requested, three blocks west of the office building he had worked at in 1995, and only one block away from the investment center he had visited in 2018 to pick up his millions of dollars.

The mall had plenty of business people hustling down the sidewalks, crossing streets with their briefcases or purses clutched in hand, oblivious to a time-traveling man standing on the corner like a lost, out-of-town visitor. Martin rotated around to get a feel—more of a reminder—of his surroundings. A suit shop was across the street—his reason for being dropped at this specific location—so he crossed and entered, a bell over the door chiming to call attention, a salesman approaching like a hungry shark before Martin had taken five steps inside.

"Good morning, sir. How may I help you today?" the man asked. He stood short and spoke in a high-pitched weaselly voice. His black hair glossed under the lights, slicked back, a thin pencil mustache to complement it.

"Good morning," Martin said, scanning the store. "I'm looking for a basic suit to change into right now and walk out with. Don't need anything fancy."

Martin couldn't recall having ever been in a suit store at any point in his life, typically buying his professional attire from department store bargain racks. The vast availability was overwhelming, and he trusted the salesman would do his best to upsell him on things he surely didn't need.

"Certainly," the man said. "My name is Gordy, and I'd be happy to get the right pieces together for you. Do you prefer neutral colors, or something more pastel?"

"I like gray suits, nothing flashy."

"Absolutely, please follow me." Gordy pivoted and dashed away, Martin taking big steps to keep up with the little man. "Is there a particular occasion? Wedding? Big Valentine's date in a couple days?"

"Just looking for another outfit for work. I work only a couple blocks down and thought I'd treat myself to a new suit before heading in for the day."

"Ahh, of course, let's have a look here. Would you mind raising your arms outward to the side?" Before he could even process the question and react, Martin watched as Gordy knelt down and ran a tape measure from the inside of his ankle up toward his crotch, making him squirm at the unexpected sensation. He was done within seconds and stood up to finish measuring from Martin's wrist to armpit. "Let me pull some items."

Gordy skimmed through the rack, pulling pants, jackets, and shirts in rapid succession. Martin looked around to see if anyone else had such an energetic employee helping them, and only spotted two other men in the whole store, one already dressed in a suit, a fedora cocked over his eyes as he browsed a spinning rack of ties. The other in a long, tan trench coat, standing next to the changing rooms.

Just me. How lucky, Martin thought.

"What do you think?" Gordy asked, holding up three suit jackets, each a different shade of gray from light to dark. Martin pointed to the darkest one, and Gordy's face lit up with joy.

"One of my favorites. The color is called gun metal. A bit aggressive of a name, mind you, but definitely a powerful color, great for delivering presentations to large groups."

It occurred to Martin that this suit was actually more than something to wear as a decoy. He'd be able to keep and deliver his victory speech while wearing it, a new look for the winning commander.

Or be buried in it, his conscience reminded.

"I give a few presentations," Martin said. "This one should work just fine."

Gordy smiled, satisfied with once again matching the perfect suit to a client in need. After another fifteen minutes of upselling ties, shoes, and a pocket square, Martin stepped out of the store and back onto the mall, ready to see Izzy for the final time, unaware that the two other customers inside were now following him.

* * *

Martin had three hours to kill until noon when he planned to make his move and bump into Izzy. He had taken a moment to find a diner and dove into a breakfast burrito much bigger than his head, and to think of how this morning had played out all those years ago.

The date was easy to remember. It was Izzy's eleventh birthday, in which she and Lela had come downtown to visit Martin before grabbing lunch as part of a fun-filled day. Martin had to work, and his earlier shift didn't allow him to take his break at a good time to meet them, leaving him to settle for a quick five-minute chat before getting off at two to join them at the movie theater for a showing of *Billy Madison*. Martin remembered this detail because he and Lela had gotten into a small argument about taking Izzy to see it, since she was right on the cusp of the age to see a comedy of that nature. Izzy had wanted to see it, and since it was for her birthday, Martin had caved in and agreed to it, so long as they waited for him to join.

His frustration that day was due to having a meeting at noon sharp, another reason he wasn't able to take the rest of the day off, as the meeting was between the CEO and Martin's team. Lela and Izzy had stopped by the office around 11:40 and talked with Martin for about fifteen minutes until he returned inside.

It was that exact moment that Martin planned to swoop in from behind, perhaps on the basis that he forgot to tell them something, and give Izzy a big hug and proper goodbye. The interaction wouldn't have any bearing on the future, and he knew he was safe from 1995 Martin who would've been staring out the window of a conference room, longing for a better life without so many restraints on his schedule.

The biggest detail he had to take a guess on was the suit. He had no clue what he had actually worn that day, but had always been a fan of gray suits and took the gamble, hoping what he purchased this morning would be close enough to not draw questions from Lela.

At 11:25, Martin paid his tab and left the diner, making his way to his office building a short walk away. He'd arrive around the same time as Lela and Izzy, but would keep his distance from the scene. It seemed like centuries ago he had driven down his block in 1996 and briefly locked eyes with himself, sending Martin speeding away while he thought his head might explode. He learned his lesson the hard way about encountering his past self, and hadn't even stuck around for the worst of it.

He bolted down the sidewalk, weaving through people taking their sweet time deciding what they wanted to eat for lunch, clogging the pedestrian traffic without a care in the world. Martin also kept his eyes bouncing around, not knowing which direction Izzy and Lela would come from, needing to avoid accidentally bumping into them too soon. He stayed across the street to reduce his chances, but couldn't be sure until he saw them.

When Martin reached the spot directly across from his office, he slipped into a narrow alleyway, keeping an eye out for himself and his family. They had met right outside the main doors, and if his memory served correctly, Lela and Izzy had arrived first.

Sweat started to moisten his palms, and his legs trembled beyond control as nerves swelled inside of his stomach. Chris, the Road Runners, and the pending fall the Revolution were nowhere to be found within his thoughts. Tension had bubbled all the way up to his throat, forcing Martin to focus on his breathing as he grew somewhat dizzy.

Hold it together. You didn't come all this way to faint in the alley.

His biggest regret from his very first trip to 1996 was not getting the chance to speak a word to Izzy. He had plenty of opportunities, but was too terrified that approaching her might cause some sort of supernatural resistance from the past. He had learned so much since then, and had a better grasp of how things worked.

His brain took a moment to process what his eyes were seeing, but the floodgates of adrenaline opened when he saw Lela and Izzy had walked right up to the front doors of the office building, staying a few steps back as they waited for Martin. His heart tried beating right out of his throat, causing Martin to swallow over and over as his throat tensed shut.

"There she is," he whispered, eyes locked on his daughter who was nineteen months away from her absurd death. She faced the building, her back to Martin, but he gazed at her long brown hair, done in a special French braid for her birthday, a couple of gift bags in hand from Lela having taken her shopping before their arrival.

All of Martin's limbs felt hollowed out as he waited, wishing he had a way to fast forward time and not have to wait in dreaded anticipation for the next fifteen minutes. But no such ability existed, at least to his knowledge, so he stepped out of the alley and took a seat on a nearby bench facing his family, still too far to be noticed.

At that moment, his past self appeared on the other side of the glass doors, a wide grin as he stepped outside where Izzy ran up and jumped into his arms for a hug. The scene made his stomach churn, and he thought he might vomit for the fourth time today. If only moments like these could be captured and stashed away to revisit later in life, all the heartache he had suffered might have been a bit more tolerable.

Martin watched them converse, trying to recall what their discussion had been about, but unable to remember so much as a word that had been spoken. His mind wasn't in the right frame for such thinking, and he kept running his hands up and down his new dress pants to wipe off the sweat that kept forming.

He waited the twenty minutes—by far the longest twenty of his life—looking around, trying to not appear like some sort of stalker to any one passing by.

When the time came, his past self bent down to hug Izzy

before leaning over to kiss Lela. They waited and watched as Martin returned inside, giving one final wave before he disappeared to his office.

"Okay, this is it," Martin whispered to himself, standing on wobbly legs, fighting to keep his balance and bowels in check. He shuffled back to the alley and dropped the shopping bag from the suit store, filled with the clothes he had arrived in, knowing Lela would certainly inquire what was in the bag that had magically appeared within the last minute.

Izzy and Lela turned from the office building and started down the sidewalk. Martin dashed toward the office doors to make sure he approached them from the correct angle. His vision pulsed in and out of focus as his eyes locked onto his daughter, his feet moving as if they had a mind of their own.

Martin started jogging, shrinking the gap between himself and Izzy, reaching an arm out as he parted his lips to call her name.

A gun fired, followed by several shrieks as a slug grazed Martin's shoulder with a deep burning sensation. The chase stopped as he bent over, hand clutched over his shoulder where a small stream of blood started oozing.

"Fuck," he snarled through gritted teeth, looking up to see Izzy and Lela sprinting away from the scene, Lela running awkwardly as she shielded Izzy's head with both arms. "No! Izzy! Lela!" His shouts never reached them and they vanished around the corner. Another gun shot rang out, sending people diving under benches, hands over their heads, while others scattered away like frightened mice. The glass behind Martin shattered, falling victim to the bullet meant for his head.

He spun around, snapping back into reality, his moment with Izzy officially gone forever, and saw the man in the trench coat across the street, standing tall with a pistol pointed at his face. He was tucked into the alley where Martin had just hidden moments ago.

Shots kept firing, and Martin ducked as he ran away, flailing for his pockets and the flask of Juice that served as his return ticket to 2020 and the jet in Winnipeg. He glanced over his shoulder once he rounded the block's corner, and saw the man sprinting toward him. That moment of separation was all he needed to grab hold of his flask, unscrew the cap, and jam a swig of the Juice into his mouth. He crawled under a doorway, people still too occupied with running to safety to notice him vanish into thin air.

Chapter 24

Martin panted for breath, sweat running down the side of his face as he stood up and stretched his legs in the confines of the jet's bathroom. He grabbed the side of the sink, staring into the mirror where he saw the tear on his suit jacket's shoulder, flesh exposed with dried blood around the mild wound.

"Holy shit," he gasped, still catching his breath. He turned on the sink and splashed some water on his face, tossing a handful on his hair to help clean up his appearance. Hopefully no one outside would question anything and think he just had a difficult time on the can. Martin patted his suit, furious he had no chance of grabbing the bag of clothes he had departed in, now lying beside a dumpster in 1995 Denver where a homeless person would surely enjoy their warmth.

His breathing was back under control, but he still drew a long breath before unlocking the door and stepping outside. Most everyone remained scattered about the jet, carrying on their conversations. No one even looked to their commander as he wriggled his way along the wall to not be seen.

Everyone except Alina, who sat in her seat next to Martin's, an inevitable encounter awaiting him thanks to the look of judgment in her eyes. He dropped into his seat and quickly opened his laptop in hopes of giving an appearance that nothing out of the ordinary had happened. Especially a trip into the past where someone—obviously a Revolter—tried to assassinate him.

This area of the jet was equipped with a curtain that ran on a rounded track from the ceiling, meant to give the commander and lieutenant a private meeting space. They hadn't used it once, but Alina now stood up and snapped the curtain closed around them, whispering. "Where the *fuck* did you go?!"

Martin frowned, years removed from the once lethal poker face he had in his mid-20's. "To the bathroom," he said in a *how-dare-you-question-me* tone.

"And you decided to change into a suit before heading out for this mission?"

Martin felt his face flush with hot blood. He had covered the tear on his shoulder as best he could, so far relieved that she hadn't questioned it, but also knowing he had been caught.

"Commander, we all heard you throwing up this morning. I know there is no reason for you to have been in that bathroom for *ten minutes*. Tell me where you went. You could have jeopardized this entire mission." She glared into his eyes, and the tension forced him to look away and avoid eye contact. "Did you go back to see Sonya?" she hissed.

Martin shook his head, lowering it as he settled on staring to the ground. "I'm sorry. I've been thinking about my death all day and night. I went back to see my daughter one last time. 1995. I had a specific day in mind that I thought would be perfect."

Alina leaned back, but her arms remained stiff and perched on the armrests. "Did it not go well?"

Martin shook his head, still refusing eye contact. He reached up and flipped back the flap from his tattered suit, revealing the

169

bruised skin that had been grazed by the bullet. "I was maybe twenty feet away from Izzy when someone started shooting. Caught me here, but that's it. Got out before anything worse happened."

"Jesus Christ, Martin, what were you *thinking*?!"

Even though they were peers, Alina had never called Martin by his first name. Her deciding to use his name in this moment showered all of her intended disappointment over Martin.

"I don't know. It's been hard sitting here all day, watching everyone act like everything is fine in the world while I'm wondering if I'll be alive tomorrow. I had to do *something,* and figured I'd try to get in a final goodbye."

Alina shook her head. "I can't say I blame you, and I know how you're feeling. Why didn't you just come talk to me? I've had countless missions where I've wondered—no, *expected*—death to finally take me away. But here I am, ready to witness history for our organization. Believe me, Commander, if I could go do this mission for you I would, but not a single one of us can help you once time is frozen."

Martin looked up, his eyes droopy with regret. "I know, and maybe that's why I'm having such a difficult time. I'm not normally afraid of Chris, but I've always had a team surrounding me. I'm *horrified* of being alone with him. It's literally a fight to the death—on his turf."

Alina nodded. "I get it. But keep in mind, he won't have quite the advantage you think. Sure it's his cabin, but it's not like he knows the area as well as Barrow. If this encounter were taking place at his mansion, that's a different story—you'd have no chance. But this fight in the woods is probably as neutral of a site we could ask for. That's why our first step was getting him out of that mansion and demolishing it. Same with the store. Those were two locations he knew like the back of his hand. We didn't know where he'd end up going after that, but I'd say this has worked out in our favor. And there's nothing to worry about. The fact that he hasn't made an appearance confirms—at least for me—that he is indeed growing weaker since Sonya died. If he had anywhere near his regular strength he'd have made an appearance to egg you on, perhaps taunt you into making a bad decision."

Martin chuckled. "Apparently I can do that all on my own. I can't believe I just left here with no sort of protection around me. What the hell was I thinking?"

"That's beside the point now. The Chris you'll be meeting in the woods is not the one you've known this whole time. He's weak, slow, and fragile. He'll have an advantage based on position and will probably try to kill you with traditional means like a gun. If you can lure him out of the cabin, you'll have the upper hand. It's imperative that you think critically before every single step you take, play it from all possible angles before committing to a decision."

"I get that. Really. I'm not lacking confidence in our plans or even my ability to carry out this mission. It's just Chris. Even if he's weak, he has been nothing but unpredictable as long as I've known him. He's a lunatic. And do we really think he's just sitting in that cabin waiting for the time to pass? If I know him, then he's making plans as well, ready to counter whatever comes his way. Ready to kill."

"He's gonna put up a fight. I expect nothing less. This is his very existence at stake, and that of the Keeper of Time status. No one actually knows what happens when the acting Keeper is murdered, but we have teams ready to raid all of his known properties and Revolution offices across the continent to search for those answers. They will literally be barging into those places as soon as we get word that he's dead, likely during your victory speech."

"I hadn't realized that was planned. You've covered all our bases once again. I have to know—are there plans in place in case Chris wins this battle?"

Now Alina was the one avoiding eye contact, staring to the curtains enclosing them. "Of course. Not plans you'd like to hear about—no need to pollute your mind with any more doubt."

"As Commander, I demand you tell me the plans," Martin said sternly, his turn to glare at the lieutenant.

Alina shifted in her seat, clearly seeking a way out of this conversation, but running into the brick wall of a fact that Martin was indeed the highest-ranking official, and what he said had to be honored. She cleared her throat. "There are two scenarios we have planned for aside from a victory. The first one is an unlikely possibility that both you and Chris end up dead. Should that happen, I'll become the commander, and Arielle has agreed to be my lieutenant. We will move forward with the rest of the plan after a month-long memorial in your honor."

"Wow, so you already know how long my funeral will be," Martin said, forever impressed by the level of planning.

"It won't come to that, we just have to be prepared for every possibility. The second scenario is one where you die and Chris lives. The plans for that will be to disband the North American Road Runners and allow our members to hide away in a remote location since we won't be able to offer any sort of protection. We'd be closing the doors on the organization forever."

Martin's eyebrows shot up. "You wouldn't keep fighting?

How can that be?"

"Commander, you asked me to lead this mission. I've had the late-night meetings with people from every corner of the organization and have run these plans by everyone, including the other commanders and yourself—minus these particulars. The consensus is that this is our final chance to kill Chris. A *real* chance. We've never been this close. Never has a Road Runner sat a couple hundred miles away from Chris, with a real opportunity to take his life. Almost fifty years of existence. If this mission fails, then we believe the organization will fail with it. No more excuses, no more second chances. Just an acceptance of the reality that we'll never beat Chris at his own game."

"So you'll let me die in vain," Martin said, more to himself. "Interesting. I suppose this isn't the organization I thought."

Martin stood as if to leave, but Alina shot her hand out, grabbing his forearm and urging him to sit back down. "Commander, please."

He paused a moment, locking eyes with her and debating everything from storming out of the curtains, to resigning as commander and running away forever. Begrudgingly, he sat down and crossed his arms. "Go ahead."

"This isn't a decision we just threw together for the sake of discussion. It was calculated and considered, even the Council reviewed it and had quite the heated debate. Eventually, everyone involved came to an agreement that should we lose a commander for the second time this year, then we're probably not meant to stay in operation. Your death would only spark further division and fear, and the organization would likely fizzle away on its own because of it. None of this is ideal, but we felt it was the right decision."

Martin rubbed his temples. He had always known he was responsible for the lives of millions of Road Runners, but this mission now seemed as direct of a correlation as any, bringing back the grueling sickness to his entire body.

"I didn't realize any of this—you should have told me. I'd have had a different mindset during these past few weeks. Why wouldn't you tell me that our very existence depended on this mission?"

Alina shrugged. "I thought that already seemed pretty obvious, and we didn't want to add any more pressure. We're well aware of the risk and severity of what we're asking you."

Martin shook his head. "I think you're forgetting. No one asked me to do anything. This mission was my idea, you just figured out the details. I've been on board with everything you've proposed and will continue to be. Don't worry about scaring me and be honest, that's all I want."

"I will—I'm sorry. How are you feeling?"

Martin drew a deep breath and blew it out of his mouth. "This is a lot to process, but I'm ready. I can't say it's necessarily changed how nervous I am about going into those woods. I'm going to need to face the music at some point, regardless of how much I drag out the next few hours."

"You know what the best way to pass time is?" Alina asked, prompting a shrug from Martin. "Conversation. We've already been behind this curtain for twenty-five minutes. How about you and I go around the jet and just check in with everyone on this fabulous team? It'll lead to some small talk, help keep your mind off things while we pass the time."

"Okay, let's give it a try."

They both rose this time, and Alina pulled back the curtains, pleased to find no one attempting to eavesdrop. They walked together, striking up conversations with everyone who had made this mission possible, Martin unable to help but steal glances at his watch, the final countdown now underway.

Chapter 25

As expected, Alina's plan worked flawlessly. Martin caught up with people he hadn't chatted with since their initial flight to Chicago three weeks ago. The talks provided plenty of distraction, but weren't quite enough to completely erase the pending doom from his mind, much like his brief mission to see Izzy had succeeded in doing before spiraling out of control.

One jet window had been left open to provide a glimpse of the outside world, the rest ordered to remain shut for security reasons. Martin had watched the afternoon pass, the bright glow from outside giving way to a soft orange haze as the sun descended on the cold autumn night. 5:15 arrived, and with it came the group of four Road Runners who had ventured out earlier in the day to drive the exact route that Martin was about to endure.

Felix Francisco was the first one to step through the doorway, a rather short man of pale complexion, his dirty blonde hair ruffled as if they had driven all 400 miles with the windows down.

"Everything looks clear," he said, making his way toward Alina and Martin. "Even the construction zone has been cleaned up. It's a straight shot to Angle Inlet, no slowdowns, no speed traps, and not even a border checkpoint."

"Thank you, Felix," Alina said, grinning proudly. "We knew about the border crossing not having any sort of checkpoint, but I'm very pleased to hear the construction is out of the way. This should allow plans to move ahead just slightly from our projected schedule. Commander Briar, you can leave now if you'd like, since there aren't any adjustments to be made."

The dread of hearing those words suffocated Martin as he faked a smile, nodding his head by sheer will. "Okay. I'm ready."

The jet fell silent as everyone realized the moment had finally arrived. Arielle worked her way from the rear cabin, a backpack slung over one shoulder as she approached Martin's side. They shuffled toward the jet's open doorway, pausing as Martin faced the team. "Thank you all, again. None of this would be possible without you. Regardless of what happens, my only hope is that the legacy of your hard work will live forever."

"Give him hell, Commander!" someone shouted, but Martin's mind was too busy racing to notice who. Everyone else broke into cheers, showering him with well wishes and good luck. He waved one final time before following Arielle down the steps where an all-black SUV waited below, picked up and dropped off by the crew who had just returned.

The outdoor air refreshed Martin, the cold filling his lungs a much needed change of pace from the stuffy jet. The silence immediately added to the sense of solitude that he had been mentally preparing for. The next two hours would be just him and Arielle; after that, just him and Chris.

"You ready, Commander?" Arielle asked once they reached the bottom of the stairs. He lugged a duffel bag over his shoulder, pulling it off to toss in the backseat.

"Yes," he replied, more to hear himself confirm he was ready for this mission. They both climbed into the vehicle, Arielle firing up the engine and punching their destination into the car's GPS system.

Martin watched as the map calculated their route, drawing a thick blue line that curved downward and to the right before breaking further south where the image of a checkered flag signified their final destination.

Arielle shifted the car into gear and pulled out of the hangar without another look back, zipping out of the airport as if they were running late instead of early, driving like she wanted this trip over with as much as Martin.

"Consider this time yours, Commander," she said. "If you want music, want to talk, or want complete silence, just say the word."

"I'd be lying if I said I know what I want. What do you normally do before a tense mission?"

"Personally, I hype myself up in the mirror, remind myself that I'm the best, and usually blast the radio. I've never had much time to sit down and organize music, pick out my favorite songs and what not, so I just listen to what's on."

"Let's try that. Not too loud—I'm not trying to have a headache by the time we get there."

Arielle giggled. "Of course not, I wouldn't blast it too long. Keep in mind my mission prep is normally a few minutes, not a whole two hours."

She powered the radio from the steering wheel controls, getting static at first, then pressing through to other stations until finding one she liked with The Weeknd singing something about blinding lights—Martin wasn't sure.

Arielle bobbed her head as they reached the freeway, not afraid to drive 90 miles per hour as they sped away from

Winnipeg. Martin watched her dance in her seat, envious of how much joy she seemed to have under the circumstances. Watching her reminded him of Izzy, and what she might have been like if still alive today. She too loved music and singing, dancing around the living room and down the hallway just to get a laugh from Martin and Lela. Those memories seemed like an entirely different lifetime, and Martin supposed maybe humans did have multiple lives during their time on this planet, always one tragedy away from changing the trajectory of their future.

He pulled out his wallet and flipped it open to the picture of his daughter. Arielle might be the one taking him to the mission, but Izzy would be the one to take him *through* it, and, hopefully, to the finish line. He tried his best to make this mission personal, even though it was much bigger than him. A world without Chris or a Revolution just might allow him to safely travel back in time and have the encounter with Izzy that he so desperately desired. The thought of those bullets firing at him in 1995 was enough to stir up the rage within, bringing with it a renewed desire and dedication to see this mission through its end.

The song ended and the radio station took a commercial break, causing Arielle to lower the volume as she continued down the freeway like a drag racer.

"I didn't realize that driving was one of your strong suits," Martin said. "Do you have any actual weaknesses?"

"I love driving, and no I do not," she replied with a soft chuckle. "After I lost my family, I dedicated my entire life to the Road Runners and being the very best. We don't have any certifications because we don't believe in that sort of stuff, but we get graded, us agents. Sort of like power rankings. I've

179

been number one for the last two years, and was number two behind Alina until she started taking fewer missions to work on bigger projects. My scorecard shows no weaknesses either. I've earned perfect marks in driving, running, strength, stealth, espionage, shooting, bombs, combat, and a whole bunch of other categories I can't keep track of."

"Christ. And you were trained under the Road Runners like anyone else?"

Arielle nodded. "Yes, the program is great. What you put in is what you'll get out. I'd skip days off and do more training on my own. When sessions ended, I stayed and worked in private with the instructors. And I don't want you to think that the rest of our agents are lazy or don't care, they're all fantastic—I just wanted so much more out of it. Training became like a drug for me, it gave me a high. Then when I graduated from training, missions gave me a new high. Then it was the agent rankings, and I wanted to climb all the way to the top. I literally can't get enough of this work."

"So driving me two hours is pretty boring work for someone like you?"

"Not at all. There is no higher honor than working on a mission for the commander. And this one is working *with* the commander. It might not be as physically grueling as other missions, but it's definitely the most important mission I've ever been assigned."

"You're an impressive young woman," Martin said. "When I was your age, I was drinking every night in college, just trying to get by with C's to graduate. Even with what you've been through you know exactly what you want out of life and how to get it. I am curious, though, where do you go from here? You're the top-ranking agent, so what is left to achieve for Arielle

Lucila?"

"I honestly don't know. I've enjoyed being the top agent and I definitely want to do it a few more years. I'm aware that one day I'll no longer be the best, but until then I'm going to enjoy every minute of it. I don't see myself ever entering a leadership type role—I need to be out in the world, not calling shots from behind a desk. Maybe that will change once my body has taken the abuse of this job, but maybe not. Right now, it's hard to imagine doing anything else."

"I wish I understood. It seems for me that what I've wanted out of life has constantly been in flux. I never imagined myself here, but there's no turning back now."

"I believe we are always right where we need to be. I've never questioned that for a moment. At some point in our lives, we are called to fulfill our destiny. Most people shy away—it's the spectacular ones who step up. It's important we never doubt ourselves."

Martin had never considered anything about his life to be spectacular, but the sentiment still managed to consume his thoughts as they sped along. He didn't respond, and Arielle seemed content letting her remarks linger as they continued without further conversation, the radio playing softly and Martin coming to terms with fulfilling his own destiny.

Chapter 26

Arielle was skilled in several categories, as she had mentioned. Relaxing a flustered person was nothing difficult for her, even if it was the commander of the Road Runners. She'd found herself in plenty of scenarios, as a group leader, having to rein in the erratic emotions of her team as they embarked on extraordinarily risky missions, lives teetering on the brink of death for each grueling second.

Commander Briar fell more on the charts as a man who couldn't get out of his own head. He put up his own roadblocks of doubt as the mission progressed from its initial days as a mere idea.

Arielle didn't care. Her job was to get the commander safely to Angle Inlet where he'd wander into the woods on his own. Safely was the key word, and that also applied to his mental capacity. If he were to have any fighting hope of actually bringing down Chris Speidel, no matter how weak all reports claimed the monster to be, he needed a clear, focused mind. Arielle had stalked Chris for nearly the entirety of his life as they sought to learn his vulnerabilities as the Keeper of Time. She was perhaps the Road Runner with the most knowledge of what Chris was capable of. She knew his burning desire to keep his power and status, a willingness to stop at no costs to protect it. He had even admitted in a private conversation with his lifelong friend, Duane, that he would indeed kill his own daughter if it meant staying in control.

She had no way of knowing what Chris was up to at this exact moment as they drove through the middle of the Manitoba province, but she could guarantee that the Keeper of Time was indeed making preparations for Martin's arrival. The chaos around the country certainly tipped off the fact that Chris was worried. If he had any confidence in his ability to come out of this situation alive, there wouldn't have been any need for such deliberate distractions.

This fact had been obvious to both her and Alina, and they assumed to Commander Briar, but they had no way of knowing for sure. The commander had a tendency to close off his emotions and thoughts, sometimes becoming distant in the middle of meetings and conversations. Alina assured her he was a calculated person, not afraid to take his time and examine a situation from all perspectives before blurting out an idea. Knowing this, she had drilled it into his head during the drive that he must act exactly that way once entering the woods.

"Don't think this is a matter of just walking up to his door and knocking," she said once the festive mood of blaring music died down and they came within the final thirty minutes of their destination.

"Nothing has ever been simple with Chris," Commander Briar replied. "Even when he and I were on the same side."

"Even if he's been weakened, expect him to use powers we haven't seen. This is the final stand, and the entire time travel world knows what's at stake. I'm not sure if the lieutenant has mentioned it, but your name is splattered across the news—well, it was before the blackout. Road Runners aren't

183

dumb. They know what's going on and the anticipation is causing madness—pretty sure that's what led to all the protests."

Commander Briar raised his hand. "Please, Arielle. I'm well aware of the stakes and the stress our entire organization is under. I intend to put an end to it, but you know what's been a calming realization that I haven't had until this car ride? The fact that if I fail, I don't have to be around to deal with the consequences. Maybe it's morbid to think that way, even negative, but it has brought a sense of calm that I've been struggling to find all along."

It's called acceptance, Arielle thought, knowing that the removal of fear was one more pillar to fall that had been holding up the commander's self-doubt. She understood the fine line between fearless and reckless, and the former always led to stunning results on her mission work.

"I don't think it's morbid at all," she said, taking a sip of water and putting the bottle back into the cupholder separating them. "And it's not negative—it's *positive*. You're setting yourself up for success, but what do I know? I'm no psychiatrist."

She grinned, knowing that even though she had no degree in psychiatry, she had taken the same courses and had an equal understanding as someone practicing in the field, just another weapon in her never-ending arsenal. This moment wasn't anywhere in the plans—especially the long drive—but she had been told by Alina to prepare for it nonetheless. Commander Briar would need to be convinced that he could defeat Chris, but he'd just need a little mental nudge to get him to believe it himself. The car ride provided ample time to get the job done, and she sensed a shift in both his tone and body language compared to when they had first left Winnipeg.

"Can I ask you for a favor?" Commander Briar in a hushed voice. "Not as your commander, but as a concerned citizen."

"Okay," Arielle said, bracing herself for an odd request.

"If I die, I need someone to fight these plans to abolish the Road Runners. It's wasteful, and while I understand the basic logic behind it, I think it's highly irresponsible of our organization to stop when it's all so close. If it were up to me, my death should be followed with a quick attack. Don't worry about my body—if you get a chance to drop bombs on this cabin to end the war, then do it."

"First off, you're not going to die, so stop thinking like that. Secondly, I don't have enough power to do anything like that."

"Then start a new group. Take the Road Runners who are interested in continuing the fight and finish it. Don't let me die for no reason."

Arielle shook her head, becoming distracted by her simple task at hand, not wanting to lose the momentum of confidence that had been brewing within Commander Briar. "The lieutenant made this decision and already stomped out this possibility. She said if anyone gets caught trying to continue, they will be detained by the Road Runners. Trips are already booked for tonight in case the worst happens; they want to move quickly with our departure, so Chris or any of his Revolters don't have a chance to track us down before they realize what's happening."

"Trips? What about everyone on the jet? This team who has given everything for this mission... they're just going to fly away in the night?"

Arielle nodded. "We've each booked a flight to our preferred location—safe zones scouted out by the organization, with a lot of help from Councilman Templeton." She debated dropping that name in front of the commander, unsure how he'd react seeing as Templeton ran against him for the commandership. He remained smug, arms crossed with a look of disappointment stuck on his face.

"Where are you flying to?" he asked, monotone.

"Europe. Small island off the coast of Greece. Traveling outside of North America was strongly encouraged, so that's what most of us decided."

Martin snorted. "Funny. All I've wanted was a vacation, but it's been one thing after another, even before becoming commander. The one vacation I took—which was to clear my head after Chris slaughtered my mother—was soon interrupted and I had to run. Do you know how many times I've thought about running away to an island, or Europe, just to get away from this life? Running against Templeton—who, quite frankly, I loved his idea of running away. And now to hear that is *literally* the plan for all Road Runners should I die." He jerked his head from side to side, biting his bottom lip to the point of nearly drawing blood. "What a fucking slap in the face."

Arielle had completely lost control of the commander and felt as if they were back to square one, if not even regressed from that point. The GPS showed only fifteen more minutes until they arrived. "Look, Commander, we can bicker about these decisions all you want, but we're about to arrive and there will be no turning back. Everything has been planned and arranged to ensure your success on this mission. I'm sorry how things have unfolded, but this is where we are. The finish line is literally at the end of this road. It's time to block out the noise and get ready for what's coming."

Commander Briar turned his head away and looked out of the passenger window, the glow from the dashboard lights brightening his face in the reflection. Arielle noticed him staring blankly into the pitch-black of the woods. "I'm fine—really. I've been waiting for this moment for a very long time. It's just all these logistics behind the scenes keep me distracted. I know they shouldn't, but I've really grown to appreciate my role in leading this organization. The thought of it no longer existing, regardless of the circumstances, really fires me up."

"Then win." Arielle spoke these two words sharply, watching as they stabbed Commander Briar in the gut of his psyche.

"Then win," he repeated, nodding his head. "Well, if you say so, then that's what I'll do." He grinned, the tension softening within the car.

"The key to my success has been to trust my teams that plan the missions. If you're confident in who you hired on this team, then there is no reason to not trust and follow their directions. You're equipped with everything you need, just follow the plan."

The road changed from pavement to dirt, signifying that they were now five minutes away from their destination. Arielle knew this, the GPS showed it, but Commander Briar said nothing, not even looking toward the center console that confirmed these details.

"It's time to call Steffan," Arielle said, keeping her voice soft with hopes of not startling her commander any more.

He pulled out his cell phone and started dialing, Arielle listening intently, nerves starting to formulate, intimidated by the sheer magnitude of this ultimate step in the mission.

"Mr. Privvy," Commander Briar said in a forced, cheerful voice. "How are things there at such a late hour?" He nodded while Steffan replied from across the Atlantic, finally looking at the GPS. "Yes, looks like we are three minutes away. So give me five on top of that and you'll be all set to freeze it. Eight minutes total from right now." He gulped and looked back out his window, his legs bouncing uncontrollably. "Ninety minutes, understood. I'd better be done well before that. Thank you."

The commander hung up and let out a deep sigh, keeping his eyes closed as the inevitable had finally arrived. "It's all taken care of," he said. "I'll be staying in the car with you to confirm when time is frozen, then I'll head into the woods."

"Understood, sir," she said with a quick nod as the car slowed down and pulled to the side of the road, the little strip of shops roughly two hundred yards ahead of them. Arielle killed the engine and turned off the headlights, leaving them to listen to the howling wind outside, blowing swirls of snow from the tops of the surrounding trees.

Arielle had never knowingly gone into frozen time, the act not having an effect on those not involved. From her vantage point, time would continue as it was, the pause passing in a matter of milliseconds within her mind, while Commander Briar used the next ninety minutes of frozen time to roam the woods. Only he, Chris, Steffan, and any other lucky Warm Souls alone could use the world as a playground.

The commander checked his watch. "Should be one or two minutes until he freezes it. I'll see you on the other side."

Arielle didn't know what further to say, relieved to not only see, but *hear* the regained confidence in Commander Briar's voice. "I'll be right here, ready to help carry his dead body."

The commander grinned, and shot his hand to the door handle, clearly anxious and ready to dash through the dark woods as his legs hadn't stopped bouncing for the past hour. Arielle debated suggesting that he relax his body, that even a subconscious movement like his could still fatigue him before reaching the cabin. She decided against it, as starting any sort of discussion at this point would prove useless.

Arielle didn't see herself with her lips parted, her thoughts stuck in her head. Nor did she see Commander Briar step out of the car, gently close the door behind him, and start trudging into the woods.

Time had been frozen, and while no one realized it, the time travel world waited in grave anticipation.

Chapter 27

Chris Speidel lay on the bed in his cabin, drenched in sweat, shivering as he patted himself dry with the couple of hand towels kept in the place. He had confirmed that he was officially on his own, with no invincibility to save his life. *I have to do it myself,* he thought.

He had spent the past hour channeling the abilities afforded to him as the Keeper of Time, but little did he know—he did, but his arrogance refused to let him accept reality—every task he had ever done as Keeper expelled a certain amount of energy from his body. While invincible, however, that fatigue was never noticed. With that protection now removed, and combined with his archaic age, Chris found himself forced to choose with careful precision how to best proceed. His first priority was to enter the mind of Martin Briar to learn his foe's whereabouts.

Much to his surprise—he didn't think Martin would come so soon—he entered Martin's mind to find him in a car, headed toward Angle Inlet, Minnesota, with a beautiful young woman driving the vehicle. The act of entering Martin's mind had drained Chris, knocking him on his ass for five minutes after returning to his own conscience. Once he regained some strength, Chris dashed outside to confirm the slots in his cabin walls had unobstructed views to all surrounding angles. He returned inside where he further prepared for the impending encounter, placing boxes of ammunition in different positions, leaving him free to reload his guns wherever he ended up within the confined space.

Chris debated trying different tactics available to him as the Keeper, but didn't want to lose what little energy he had left in the tank. It was a double-edged sword. Should he decide to fight Martin as a mere mortal man, he'd have better endurance and would only have to wear Martin out. He didn't know which direction Martin would come from—he was still too far to tell—and he didn't want to waste energy moving from wall to wall until his old friend arrived. So he gambled and settled in the cabin's southeast corner, also convenient as that is where the bed was, providing a soft seat for Chris while he waited. He figured Martin would either enter the woods from the airport or the town. The airport would require him to backtrack, while the town was the first option when driving in.

The lack of communication to the outside world drove Chris crazy. He wanted to know how the riots around the continent were going, and if they had changed anything. Clearly the Road Runners didn't care since Martin was still on his way, but the fact that he was coming with only one other person suggested resources were thin. He knew the odds were lined up for time to be frozen, something even the Keeper of Time had no way of controlling should someone else authorize the act. He could try freezing time first, but that action required an amount of energy from Chris that could kill him.

After racking his brain for the past half hour, he decided on a crafty maneuver that he hadn't used in years. Always focused on big picture decisions, and not so much with the happenings of individual time travelers, Chris had long lost the need he hoped would now serve as a final resort in throwing Martin off his game.

The plan was to re-enter Martin's mind, knowing the cost would again drain him of the ability to move for a few minutes. He wasn't returning to see where his enemy was—it had already become clear where he was headed—but to play with his emotions and thoughts. Chris could extract memories from one's mind and tinker with them to the point of driving his victims mad. For Martin, he knew he could make the voices of his mother, daughter, wife, and even Sonya, play within his skull. With a little extra push, he could create a visual hallucination of them, something that would surely drive Martin to madness.

Having just been in Martin's head, Chris had a better sense for what to expect as far as the toll these actions would take on his body. It fortunately didn't require much more than his first dip into the waters. Once inside someone's mind, it became like roaming an open-world setting and deciding what to do. The biggest gamble was deciding the best time to re-enter Martin's mind, knowing if he went too soon, his actions could fall wasted if Martin was merely sitting in a car. And if he waited too long, Martin would arrive to the cabin before Chris had an opportunity to sway him. He needed to leave Martin flustered upon his arrival to the woods, completely frazzled by the time he reached the cabin.

Chris had no familiarity with the roads driving into Angle Inlet, but he could tell Martin was within at least thirty miles, judging by the glimpse of surrounding trees he had caught. That had been an hour ago, and if Martin hadn't yet arrived to the cabin, then he either had to be walking through the woods, or sitting at their outer edge, regardless of the direction he decided to enter from.

"No time like the present, as they say," Chris said to his empty room. He lay on the bed, folding his hands over his stomach as he closed his eyes and prepared his mind for the grueling task of re-entering Martin's conscience. The process was similar to an intense meditation session, Chris assuring his mind was clear, aligned with his breathing as he maneuvered to get it all in perfect harmony.

Chris drew a long, deep breath, the stuffy cabin air filling his lungs that had aged fifty years in the past day. He cleared his mind, sifting through and pushing away the thoughts of war, the chaos around the continent, and narrowing the entirety of his concentration on his target, Martin Briar. He started down the hallways of his subconscious, knocking upon all the doors that served as portals into the minds of those lives he had welcomed to the wonderful world of time travel. Millions of them. But the hallway knew his greatest desires, and wouldn't make him run down the thousands of miles of doors decorating each side. It would know to bring Martin's door to the front.

And it did, right after tempting Chris with the opportunity to take a peek into Duane's mind and see what his old friend was up to at this exact moment. He shook his head. "No time, I'm afraid."

The doors were labeled with each person's name in simple gold lettering. After ten steps he found the one belonging to Martin Briar and wasted no time turning the shiny knob and entering, the sensation a free fall until he crash-landed in Martin's brain, watching the world through his eyes.

"Oh, yes," Chris giggled. "Finally something going my way."

Through Martin's eyes, he saw Main Street before being spun

around for a view of the woods. A car sat behind him, the lady driver appearing frozen as her eyes gazed out the windshield, lifeless and glossy.

"You son of a bitch," Chris muttered to himself. "Freezing time already, before we even get to dance. I have some tricks up my sleeve, too." Chris knew that at this point in the process, his thoughts would echo in Martin's mind, like a distant narrator telling a story from the depths of the subconscious.

Through the windows of Martin's eyes, the snowy ground passed by in a white blur as he started picking up pace.

"So rushed," Chris said, refocusing on the task at hand, having to set aside his temporary glee for the turn in fortunate events. He had Martin in the precise moment he had hoped, ready to make the man's trek through the woods a living hell. He prepared to deliver the performance of a lifetime, knowing his life hung in the balance of the next thirty minutes.

He briefly attempted to take control of Martin's mind and body, a task he had never quite mastered, and doubted he had the energy to complete now. He felt the momentary grip around Martin's conscience, promptly slipping through his fingers like a wet fish.

Chris backed off and settled for the barrage of mental attacks he had enqueue, letting the world and Martin's subconscious fall silent as he hid in the corner, ready to fight.

Chapter 28

Martin started into the woods, dragging his feet as he kept shooting glances over his shoulder, convinced Chris had somehow planted another Warm Soul to tail him. But no one appeared, and the reality settled in that it truly was Martin and Chris, alone in the wilderness to fight to the end.

Much to his surprise, Martin didn't feel the weight of the world on his shoulders as he crunched through the patches of snow, following a hand-drawn map that showed the safest path to the cabin. He couldn't even acknowledge the gravity of the situation after stressing over this exact moment all day. The thoughts of death and the jumble of scenarios for how this could all play out remained dormant in his mind, his eyes focused on the physical steps ahead.

He did as advised, taking one step at a time, staying behind one of the several tree trunks that surrounded him, shielding him from the outside world where no one would ever hear his screams. Chris had proven a deliberate man, and Martin didn't doubt this location was part of a long series of well-calculated decisions should matters escalate to this point.

Remember, Martin reminded himself. *You're on* his *land. It's all designed to give him an advantage. Be ready for anything. Bear traps, trees falling over. A split-second decision can decide your life in these woods.*

With that thought, the adrenaline started to pump into his veins. Looking ahead, Martin observed trees as far as he could see, snow scattered in the few areas that lacked foliage high above. Any sighting of a cabin waited at least fifteen minutes ahead, possibly more if he took a wrong turn. But he trusted the map would guide him with no issues.

He continued forward, hiding from something he couldn't see, trusting the process and his own abilities to save the world while it remained frozen. He imagined Commander Blair, surely pacing his office in London, flipping desks and furniture over in a fit of rage once he realized time had been frozen without his knowledge, assuming he was awake at the odd hour. To Martin and Steffan's knowledge, Commander Blair didn't know any other Warm Souls besides himself and Martin. If he was sleeping—something Martin now understood as a rare commodity for commanders—then he'd wake to news of one story or another, leaving the fact that time had been frozen irrelevant.

Martin shook his head, refusing to fall down the rabbit hole of what-ifs, especially in a situation where a bullet could strike him without warning should he lose focus. He resumed watching his feet, looking to the ground, then up to the nearest tree to hide behind.

A woozy sensation swarmed over him for a brief moment, and he thought he heard Chris's voice speaking in his head. But it wasn't loud or clear enough to make out for certain. He stopped in his tracks to listen to the silent world around him. No animals, no chirping bugs, no distant hum of vehicles driving around town. The silence echoed back to him and he took one more step before stopping again.

"Martin," a soft voice said, one that sent chills across his whole body. A voice that made his heart pound with the drums of love.

"Sonya?" he asked to the wilderness, his voice carrying.

"Oh, Martin," Sonya's voice replied, echoing, cocooning around him, prompting him to spin to find the source. "We could have had a life together. Was this all worth it? Why did you let me die?"

"That's a lie!" Martin growled, his lips quivering as he kept jumping around in place, hands sprawled in front of him as if he were ready for an attack. Deep down he knew that Sonya's voice wasn't real, and it had to be a decoy from Chris, but that didn't stop him from wanting to lean into this moment and see where it might take him.

"You didn't kill me, but I'm dead because of you. You should have never kept looking for me—I'd still be alive."

Martin cupped his hands and slapped them over his ears like a child throwing a tantrum. He wanted to see if the voice was in his head or actually occurring in the woods. "Sonya, where are you?"

"Buried where you instructed—right next to Izzy." The voice spoke from the trees, muffled through his hands, its lingering echo still shooting around him when he lowered them back in front of his body.

"None of this was supposed to happen," Martin said. "I just wanted to live a normal life with you. I had no control over how things played out. I was sucked into this."

"You were always in control, Martin. You were on the beach in the Bahamas. You could've stayed. Could've arranged for a boat to pick you up and take you away before those two guards had a chance to realize what was happening. You could have stayed in 1996. You could have accepted your mother's fate and not traveled into the future. There were so many actions you could have taken—or not taken—to change the course of your life."

Martin lowered his arms, no longer fearful of a potential attack, recognizing the mind games Chris was playing instead.

"I can't change anything now—all I can do is keep moving forward."

Martin took his own advice, emotions swirling no differently than the snow above him before time had frozen, and continued walking, still aware to remain behind the trees as he checked the trembling map clutched in his grip.

"I'll forever be the one you think about, Martin. I only hope you can find peace, no matter how this turns out for you."

He kept walking, shaking his head and fighting back tears. He had been too emotionally scarred to let something like this distract him. His heart had hardened over the years, even more so since joining the world of time travel.

Sonya's voice kept speaking, but mostly remained in the area behind him, unable to follow him as only the echoes remained. *That's it,* he thought. *That's all he could throw at me and it didn't work.*

"Marty," a new voice called out, freezing Martin where he stood behind the next tree trunk.

"No," Martin cried, leaning back on the tree as his legs grew wobbly. "None of this is real."

"Everything is real, Marty," said the voice of Marilyn Briar. "I might not be here physically, but I *am* real. As real as the stars in the sky, or the dead leaves beneath your feet. I'll always watch over you."

Martin regained his strength, fully aware Chris was putting

him through these auditory hallucinations, refusing to succumb to the emotional tailspin his rival was surely counting on.

"Nope." He kept walking, bouncing to the next tree, stomach churning as he saw the distance on his paper map shrink between him and the cabin's supposed location.

"Marty, come back!" Marilyn's voice cried. "Come back and save me. Don't fail again and let me die. Help me!"

The mere act of walking away from his mother's voice was enough for tears to start oozing from his eyes. But he pushed through, leaving her behind just like he had unknowingly done when he traveled to 2064 for her medicine.

Over the next five minutes, Martin further reduced the distance to the cabin. He hadn't looked too far into the distance, only concerned with what was immediately in front of him, but when he glanced up and saw a small figure standing between two trees, he slowed down, squinting for a better view. His heart knew who it was—or at least who it was supposed to be—but his brain offered every objection to reject what his eyes saw.

It was a young girl standing with her back to Martin, a puffy black coat draped over her body, its hood pulled over her head. Despite knowing it was a physical impossibility for his daughter to be standing in these woods, he couldn't deny how real she appeared. Still, Martin was ready for anything, even for Chris to be hiding inside that coat, sure to pounce on Martin as soon as he stood close enough.

He inched his way closer, still cognizant of the trees, but his eyes now glued ahead to the figure standing alone, not moving in the frozen time. "Izzy?" he called out, nearly inaudible as his throat had tensed with what felt like a tennis ball inside.

"Izzy?" he tried again, much louder as his voice swirled around the woods.

The girl wavered in place before taking a slow, cautious turn to face Martin. The softest of smiles touched the corners of her mouth, flooding Martin with nostalgia and grief while his heart hammered against his chest. "Hi, Daddy," Izzy said, her eyes sparkling as they always had, her hair brushed back and hidden inside the jacket's hood.

Martin tried once more to convince himself that this was fake, certainly a figment of his uncontrolled imagination. But he couldn't argue with Izzy's physical appearance in front of him, just like he had seen her hours ago during his quick trip to 1995.

Just like you see her whenever you close your eyes?

"Izzy, wh-what are you doing here? *How?*"

"Oh, Daddy, I'm always with you, right next to you. Don't you know that?"

Martin raised his eyebrows, scanning his daughter, trying to find the faintest of hints that suggested she wasn't real, a hologram, a ghost, anything besides flesh and bone. He remembered his urge to grab her during his first trip to 1996, hug her and run away where they could spend the rest of their lives in peace. That he never had the opportunity pained him over the years that had since passed. All of that followed up with the teaser of a similar chance during his most recent trip, only to be interrupted by the Revolution.

Martin briefly considered the possibility of running away with Izzy, even if this was some sort of hallucination or alternate reality. But he couldn't, not when he was minutes away from potentially ending the Revolution once and for all. His chest tightened with pain at the thought, knowing that regardless of how this ended, this would most likely be the last time he'd see Izzy. If he lived to tell about it, he'd never go back and try to find her again. If he actually managed to fulfill his destiny and cause his enemies' downfall, it was time to close all doors from the past and only look ahead to the bright, hopeful future.

"C-can I hug you?" Martin asked, not sure if the question or action were appropriate.

Izzy parted her lips in a wide grin. There were no signs of Chris lurking behind that smile—it was the real thing—and Martin stepped forward, arms stretched out as Izzy allowed herself to fall into his embrace.

Her warmth radiated Martin, Izzy's sweet scent both familiar and foreign at the same time. Alone in the woods, two long-lost souls reunited, Martin broke into hysterical crying. "Oh, my God, it's really you," he said, a hand pressing her head into his chest, squeezing her with all of the love that had never vanished.

"You need to go, Daddy. We're all watching," Izzy said, her voice muffled as she spoke into Martin's heaving chest.

"I know." He squeezed tighter, watching his tears fall on top of her hood in dark spots, fading away as soon as they landed. "I'm so sorry I wasn't there that night. I just wanted to tell you how proud I am of the person you were—the young woman you were becoming. I love you, always and forever."

Izzy pulled back, looking up to her father, Martin returning a gaze through bleary eyes, fighting his natural reaction to frown. "I love you, Daddy. You need to go, and so do I. Grandma wanted me to tell you how proud she is of you for always getting back on your feet after being knocked down, but that today isn't the day to try so hard."

Martin's brows furrowed as he digested this statement. If Chris knocked him down, you could guarantee he'd be right back on his feet to defend himself. Was his mother really calling on him from the grave to roll over and take defeat?

"I love you, Izzy, more than you'll ever know."

Izzy looked up to him, her big blue eyes filled with joy, and nodded before turning around without another word. She walked with a slow, steady pace, not in any hurry to leave, but not trying to stick around either. It took two minutes until she was completely out of sight, Martin left with nothing but memories, satisfied to have received the little bit of closure he wanted before his own potential death. Martin tried to follow her, of course, but his legs wouldn't move, destiny tugging him in the other direction.

The blanket of silence returned to swallow him up, and he pulled his map back out from his pocket to see he was well within a thousand feet of the cabin. He had no idea how much time had already passed since he had left Arielle behind. He was fairly certain the allotted time hadn't passed, but the distractions he encountered so far had a way of skewing everything about reality.

Just go. There's no time to look back.

Martin continued, forcing himself to refocus after the emotional reunion with his daughter. The encounter left him more puzzled than before. If this had all been some ploy by Chris—which it had to be—then what exactly was the purpose of Izzy being herself? Clearly the voices of Sonya and his mother were there to frazzle him, so why would Izzy be encouraging? Was she part of Chris's games, or had that been her actual spirit? He debated this matter over the next few seconds before catching sight of the cabin ahead.

Martin stopped, peeking around the tree trunk, shoving the map back into his pocket, pulling the duffel bag in front of his stomach to pull out his pistol, and cocking it after confirming it was fully loaded.

The woods couldn't have been any more silent, reminding Martin of the times he had gone into the empty church in Larkwood after hours, while his mother stopped by to help prepare and run after-hours events in the neighboring church hall.

He focused on the cabin, calculating the best route to remain behind the cover of the trees, seeing he'd need to hop around like a lost rabbit. If Chris decided to step outside, Martin would see him, and even take a shot.

That means he can shoot you, too, Martin reminded himself, his caution returning to the elevated level it had been before seeing Izzy. The thought of her still tried to force its way to the front of his mind, succeeding in random spurts, but having a line of vision to the cabin proved to be the better distraction.

"Oh, Commander," a voice called out, seeming to come from the trees themselves. "Commander Martin Briar."

There was no mistaking the cold voice as Chris, and Martin took a deep breath knowing their showdown waited moments away.

"Show yourself!" Martin howled, wanting to spin around and look for the source of the voice, but trusting that he needed to get closer to the cabin.

Chris laughed, the echo creating the sound of hundreds of lunatics giggling around Martin. For a moment, he thought it might drive him crazy, like nails on a chalkboard. "When you walked into my store two years ago, did you ever think this is where our relationship would take us? Life is quite romantic, wouldn't you say?"

His voice seemed to grow louder, not necessarily closer, as if speakers had been set up nearby to broadcast Chris. "I know you're all alone now," Martin shouted toward the cabin, continuing to inch closer. "Come out and fight me like a man."

Martin was now within fifty feet of the cabin, its wooden exterior clearly visible, but found he had approached from the rear, the front door nowhere in sight. He lunged toward the next tree trunk, a gunshot ringing out in unison, a fire seeming to ignite from his injured shoulder.

"Owwww!" Martin cried, one hand flying to the bullet wound, the other outstretched to catch himself as he fell to a patch of snow on the ground. He landed on the hidden bump of a root protruding from the earth, instantly numbing his torso. He was able to turn his head enough to see blood squirting from the wound, the bullet having lifted the crusty scab that had formed from getting shot earlier today. It made the injury appear much worse than it actually felt. He realized his gun was no longer in hand and felt around, grabbing nothing but powdery snow and mud.

Martin tried to sit up, desperate for a direct view of the cabin, but his back tightened, sending a sharp pain that made him stay down.

Today isn't the day to try so hard, he recalled his mother's words relayed through his daughter's spirit. *Always getting back on my feet after being knocked down. Not today.*

If Martin stayed on the ground, Chris would have no choice but to come outside. If he rose to his feet, the gunfire would continue, leaving Martin on the defense as he ran for his life. Chris surely made his plans based on staying inside the safety of his cabin, ready for any move Martin might throw his way, but did he have backup plans for something like this? Possibly, but there were too many unknown factors at play. He debated going as far as playing dead, letting his head roll to the side, closing his eyes, but decided it was best to see Chris, even if only through his peripheral vision.

The best play, he decided in this hurried moment, was to give the appearance of a struggle, perhaps showing that he was on the verge of death. Chris would have to come out for what he'd believe was the final kill shot. Martin wiggled his arms and legs, making sure all limbs were still accounted for despite his numb back and shoulder. All was well, and he braced for the sound of approaching footsteps, grateful for the silence as he'd be able to hear a pin drop in the distance.

On cue, the sound of a creaky, wooden door swung open, followed by the clopping of two boots. Martin lifted his head to see the cabin, but still had no view of the front door, wondering if he'd ever get the chance. The footsteps crunched on the mixture of snow and twigs on the ground.

"Commander Briar!" Chris called out, a clear smile in his voice. "What an absolute honor it is to have you here. Welcome to my humble abode."

The voice no longer boomed from the treetops, now direct from the source's mouth, but still echoing around the abandoned woods. Martin closed his eyes, forcing his senses to focus exclusively on the sounds around him, projecting a mental map as Chris made his way from the cabin roughly forty-eight feet away. Assuming Chris walked with a typical stride, that translated to forty-eight steps until he'd reach Martin.

Just let him talk. Don't engage or give him any reason to stay away.

"Did you really think you'd get the best of me?" Chris

continued. "After all I've seen, all I've *lived* through, and you thought the battle for the soul of the Revolution would end in a fistfight with you? The Road Runners have always been smart, I'll give you that, but you're just as naïve. You've destroyed my buildings and eliminated those closest to me, but here I am, still standing, ready to put an end to another useless commander. Strike was sweet, but you're no doubt going to be downright *delicious.*"

Chris cackled, Martin hearing the words but not listening, only counting the steps.

Forty-five, forty-four, forty-three. . .

"What do you suppose our little time travel world will look like after you're dead? Do we get to go through all of this again? I need to make some plans to get myself back in shape. Not sure I can last much longer in this old man's body. Maybe I'll transfer my soul to a younger person and keep living forever."

Forty-two, forty-one, forty. . .

"Imagine that beautiful world where the Road Runners no longer exist and I live forever, calling the shots, shaping the world into the image I've always envisioned."

Thirty-nine, thirty-eight, thirty-seven. . .

"No more poor people with no direction. They'll either join us or be eliminated. There will be the upper class and no one else."

Thirty-six, thirty-five, thirty-four. . .

"One class of humanity, flawless. Everyone has what they need. No one looks down on others because there will be no one to look down upon."

Thirty-three, thirty-two, thirty-one, thirty. . .

A gun clicked from Chris's direction. Martin noted it, but did not panic.

Twenty-nine. . .

Chris was close enough that Martin could now feel the old man's eyes on him. Martin rolled his head from side to side, letting out a moan to continue his appearance of a deep struggle.

Twenty-eight, twenty-seven. . .

"We've seen so many scenarios play out to lead us to the dream future we seek, and not one ever suggested an encounter like ours. It's funny, you can study a specific event thousands of different times, and never find a similar path. Time has a way of working itself out."

Twenty-six, twenty-five, twenty-four, twenty-three...

"You see, the mistake many people make in this time travel business is that they think they can alter time, or change the course of history."

Twenty-two, twenty-one, twenty, nineteen...

"Time is in charge, and while we might *think* we can make changes, time always finds a way to get what it wants."

Eighteen, seventeen, sixteen. . .

Chris chuckled. "You tried to stop Columbine, and time let you think you got away with it . . . until it roared back and killed *everyone*. Only time decides how we go, I suppose. The X-factor in nature that no one ever accounts for."

Fifteen, fourteen, thirteen...

Martin sensed his presence, knowing he had approximately six more steps until Chris would be standing at his feet. *Stay calm, trust the plan.* He wore a jacket thick enough to let him flex his back without Chris noticing, relieved to feel it working its way back from the stinger he had endured. Chris's voice grew louder thanks to the reduced distance.

"You didn't kill Sonya—time did—and for that I can't even

blame you. She was going to die one way or another. The fact that you were involved, however, is still unforgivable."

Twelve, eleven, ten...

The footsteps stopped, the two men ten feet apart as silence swirled around, the only two people in the country with any clue what was happening. Martin cracked open his eyes just enough to see a blurry Chris, his white hair the most prominent feature standing out against the dark backdrop of the trees. Chris held a pistol in his right hand, but didn't have it pointed toward Martin yet.

He took one more step, clearly taking caution. Martin could only rely on Chris's greed to spare his life. Had the roles been reversed, six bullets would already be in the old man's head and chest, but Chris couldn't resist the theatrics of a heated moment. He wanted the last word, and wouldn't rest until he got it. Martin groaned, rolling his head as if he were coming back to consciousness.

Chris took one more step closer, his figure casting a shadow from the moonlight that glowed high above. Martin had a moment to make his next move, knowing it was only a matter of time until Chris realized the shoulder injury wasn't anywhere near as serious as Martin had sold it. He opened his eyes, locking with the dark pit of shadows that had formed around Chris's face, and caught a final glance at the pistol still hanging by his side.

Now.

In one swift motion, Martin planted his elbows into the ground and nudged his body a few more inches toward Chris, shooting up his left foot that connected squarely with the pistol, sending it sailing toward the darkness that would make it nearly impossible to find.

Martin grunted as he sat up, his back still offering plenty of protest, but he powered through the pain, jumping to his feet and swinging a fist for Chris's face that failed to connect, sending Martin off-balance as he tumbled away.

"This ends now!" Chris snarled, his lips parted like a dog ready to attack.

Martin regained his footing and planted himself in place, ready to absorb the old man charging in his direction. Chris stomped two steps before lunging, his thin arms flailing in the air like sticks in a windstorm. He landed on Martin's shoulder, taking both men to the ground where they rolled in the snow, clamoring for an advantageous position.

A sharp pain tore through Martin's forearm, as he realized Chris had bitten him, tearing a small chunk of flesh away, spitting it behind him.

"Fuck!" Martin howled, grabbing his arm and rolling away, the duffel bag's strap getting tangled around his neck and throat. Chris leapt toward him once more, but this time Martin met him with a sturdy kick that connected perfectly on his ribcage, sending Chris sprawling to the side where he landed face-down in the snow, gasping for breath.

Martin flailed for the duffel bag, unzipping it and reaching inside for the first thing his fingers landed on. They found the handle to a hunting knife, a late addition to the bag that had been added after plenty of discussion on how to best equip Martin for the mission. His lieutenant had insisted on the knife, claiming that as long as the bag didn't leave Martin's side, he'd have every accessible weapon. The arguments against it were the risk it could put Martin in should he fall on the bag.

Martin had the final say, and agreed to carry the knife, now grateful for the decision as he watched Chris stumble back to his feet, gearing up like a bull ready to flatten him.

He has no idea, Martin thought, tightening his grip, knowing that if Chris still had any ability to read his mind, he wouldn't glare at him with rage-filled eyes.

Martin shouted, a maniac howl that filled the night, echoing through the woods that would have been heard in town had the residents not been frozen in place. He angled the knife toward the Keeper of Time, keeping it within the bag, and dashed forward, grunting as he watched Chris jump toward him.

The two men crashed into each other, Martin getting the wind knocked out of him in midair as Chris landed a fist squarely in his gut. Martin managed to hold control on the knife and pressed forward as hard as he could upon clashing with Chris, moments before both came crashing to the ground, rolling away from each other.

Martin tumbled as he tried to make his way back on his feet, slipping on a patch of ice, but gaining his footing, adrenaline bursting at full speed as he waited for Chris to do the same.

But the old man made no effort to stand, instead lying on his back much like Martin had earlier.

Don't fall for it, Martin assured himself. He would take none of the chances that Chris had, no desire for the vanity of an up close look at his enemy. He untangled the duffel bag strap and pulled it off, dropping it to the ground as he squatted to look through it—more like *feel* through it, amid the darkness. An extra gun had been packed, a small pistol to be used if his original one had gone missing.

Martin stood up, gun in hand as he shuffled toward Chris, writhing on the ground, hands clenched over his stomach, dark red spreading out from his sides and seeping into the white snow like spilled ink. He stayed six feet back, close enough to see exactly what was happening, but keeping a safe distance to leave time to react should Chris try to pull any final tricks out of his sleeves.

"Martin?" Chris whispered, his voice broken, defeated.

Martin gulped, taking one more step and planting his feet to not be tempted any closer. He also didn't gamble with his pistol, aiming it directly at Chris's head. "It's over. You have no more ways out of this."

Chris shivered as a stream of blood spilled from his lips. "It's over," he muttered. "Congratulations, you did it."

Martin's arms trembled, his mind running in overdrive as it attempted to process the reality in front of him.

"For all the powers you get as the Keeper of Time," Chris continued, forced strength clinging to each word, "You have no way of knowing how your life will end. You can jump into the future, free-falling through darkness like a stray astronaut, but we don't know if that means life or the world has ended. All I know is that my people will always put up a fight."

"You're wrong," Martin said. "Time travelers are good people. You're the one who has corrupted them. We will *all* live in a world of peace and collaboration, just like it was intended to be. There is no more room for your grim vision of the future; it's dying with you."

Chris tried to laugh, but it came out more like a choking sound. "Humans will always gravitate toward power, Martin... don't you know? Power is everything, and without it, you are nothing."

"Only for you. Humans are decent. They may fall into traps, but they can always find the right path. Your death will forever be viewed as the end of a dark era, one where everyone will rise from the ashes."

"Was this all worth it, Martin? Losing your mother, your daughter, Sonya... your life? All that just to kill me."

Martin pulled the trigger, blasting a slug through the center of Chris's forehead. "Yes, it was worth it," he said to the dead body. Chris's eyes gazed at the stars above, glossed over with death, his lips parted to deliver one final remark that would now remain trapped in his throat forever.

Martin emptied the rest of the bullets into Chris's head and torso, the dead body twitching as it absorbed each hit. After the echoes of gunshots faded away, the world returned to its blissful silence, Martin collapsing next to Chris as he broke into heavy sobs.

He had just saved the world from itself, but all he wanted was his old life back.

Chapter 29

Martin had to sit next to Chris's dead body for the next hour. He tried his cell phone, but as expected, it had no service to place a call to Steffan, leaving him to wait out the clock. He didn't touch Chris, watching as his face turned a light shade of gray, eyes still gazing lifelessly to the sky above, lips parted half an inch. He sat on the ground, back against a tree trunk, unable to help but grin at the sight of Chris Speidel's body lying in the snow three feet in front of him, pride brimming at the fact that the deed had been done by him.

While the world remained frozen, oblivious to what had just happened, Martin Briar was the only person to cherish this special moment, witnessing and participating in a historic moment that would forever live as one of the most important days for the Road Runners.

When time finally resumed, the cold weather rushed over Martin in the form of a whipping breeze. Frozen time had caused wind to stop, making his journey through the woods much more bearable, the air still and not quite feeling like the ten-degree temperature when they had arrived. He looked up to see a lone cloud swimming across the sky and wondered what the team was up to. They had no way of knowing when time was frozen, and would be resuming their conversations they hadn't realized stopped. Arielle would be on her way from the car, hopefully arriving within thirty minutes, as he had done.

A weight had been lifted, knowing the only person who wanted not just Martin, but all Road Runners dead, lay on the ground, now a frozen popsicle. Plenty of work remained, both in the immediate future of handling this corpse, but also long-term, as they needed to lay out what a peaceful world for the Road Runners looked like now that they no longer had a threat hovering above them.

Martin laughed, a combination of exhaustion and giddiness, still trying to comprehend the entire mission that had finally reached its conclusion. A smile remained stuck on his face, a sense of relief blanketing over him thanks to the closure he had received with Izzy. Even if it was only her spirit, she helped save his life. And the world.

He passed the time thinking back on the long ride it had been to arrive to this point, still in awe at how every event that happened within the Road Runners had been a gentle shove in this direction. His escaping the mansion in Barrow had started a chain of events that spun well out of his control. He had only been running for his life, aware of who Chris truly was, and needing to get as far away as possible.

The sound of wood snapping in the distance echoed around him, prompting Martin to jump to his feet. "Arielle?!" he shouted.

"Commander Briar!" a woman's voice shouted back, flooding Martin with relief as his wait was finally coming to a close. "I'm almost there, hang tight!"

Martin spun around, looking for Arielle, but not spotting her in the massiveness of the woods. Two minutes later, hurried footsteps approached, crunching through the snow until Arielle appeared from the south, gasping for breath as she crouched down in her bundled up attire of a puffy, bright yellow jacket and ski pants. Her eyes fell to Chris on the ground before meeting Martin, a childish smile spreading across her face.

"Oh my God, Commander Briar," she gasped. "Is that really him? Are you okay? There is blood all over you." Her eyes moved from Chris to Martin's blood-soaked shoulder.

Martin nodded, returning a grin of his own. "He's as dead as the dinosaurs—never coming back. And yes, I'm fine, just a little scratch."

Arielle took careful steps toward Chris, as if the dead body could still somehow reach up and snatch her ankles. She stood next to Martin, gaze stuck on Chris, jaw hanging open as she shook her head. "I can't believe he's dead."

Martin moved his arm over her shoulder, pulling Arielle into his embrace. "He's dead, but not gone. We know what we have to do next, and it won't be pretty. Let's enjoy this moment for what it is, but once we leave these woods, we owe it to the organization to never let an evil person rise to so much power again. The Revolution is going to raise hell at first. They might try to steal the body from us, might even start spreading propaganda that his death is fake, just to scare our members and start rumors. We must not let anything sway the new road ahead of us. We'll put out fires where needed, but I look forward to a day of no more fighting."

"You have a major speech to deliver after this is all settled, and no one will be able to be convinced away from the truth."

Martin nodded. "I'd like to think so, but I don't want to take any chances. I want his dead body behind me while I give the speech—we'll do it right from the jet if we need to. How much longer until the other two get here?''

"If all went according to plan, they should be here in the next half hour."

"And you're okay to help carry him all the way back to their van?''

She hesitated, staring to the body on the ground, looking into those eyes where evil no longer lurked. "Absolutely. Are *you* okay to carry him? That shoulder looks awful."

"Arielle, trust me when I tell you it's fine—nothing to worry about."

They stood in silence for a minute, both admiring the ultimate achievement of a dead Keeper of Time.

"Did you notice if your phone had any signal at the car?" Martin asked.

"It did. I sent a message to the lieutenant letting her know I was heading in. She confirmed the others should be here shortly."

"Perfect. I want to call Steffan when we arrive, thank him for taking this huge risk for us, then Alina to let her know the good news. I don't think I can hold it in for that whole ride back—I have to tell *someone*."

"Soon enough, Commander. One thing at a time."

As if answering his prayers, the sounds of more footsteps started carrying from the distance. Arielle cupped her hands to project her voice, shouting, "Darius! Marie! It's safe—hurry!"

Martin noticed the smile in Arielle's voice and couldn't help but think of the next several weeks, if not months, bringing more of the same from everyone he'd encounter throughout the organization. He might even earn a smile from Councilman Uribe, a tall task from the bull of a man.

"Coming!" a woman's voice called back, the footsteps

immediately breaking into a sprint, clopping on the ground like wild horses. Martin looked in the direction where Arielle had arrived from and saw two figures making their way, legs pumping as they ran through patches of snow and mud.

When they reached Martin and Arielle, the man pulled off his ski mask, shaking his head to let his flowing blonde hair breathe. The woman had done the same thing, the two matching in their attire, wide grins plastered across their faces. Martin recognized them from the jet, but couldn't recall any specific encounters with the two aside from courteous small talk in passing.

"Commander Briar," the man said, sticking his hand out. "Thank you. You have no idea how much this means to Marie and I. We are brother and sister, and lost our parents a long time ago because of Chris. Bounced around orphanages since we were little, and all we've ever wanted was some justice. You've just given it to us."

The words shook Martin. He understood the importance of what he had achieved—able to relate to it—but also appreciated the long journey the two siblings had surely endured. The road ahead would be filled with these types of heart-wrenching stories, something he'd need to emotionally prepare for. It was easy to lose sight, especially as commander, of the fact that everyone had their reasons for joining the Road Runners, no different from himself. All stories shared one thing in common: Chris Speidel ruining lives, either directly or indirectly.

"Don't thank just me . . ." Martin fished for the man's name.

"Darius," he replied, still squeezing Martin's hand with a slight tremble.

"Yes, my apologies. Darius. This was a team effort with so many moving parts. I simply sealed the deal."

Darius shook his head violently. "With all due respect, sir, you are wrong. Yes, we all played our part in making this happen—that was never the question. We've always had that willingness, every single Road Runner, but we've never had someone to rally behind quite like you."

"I don't understand. I'm just a regular guy. Two years ago I didn't even know time travel was a real thing."

"That's exactly it," Marie chimed in. "We all saw ourselves in you. Every commander we've had before has been great in their own rights, and each one flirted with ways to bring down the Revolution, but they always landed in the muddy politics of the situation, giving excuses as to why it wasn't the right time, or too risky. It was clear from the beginning that you were truly in this to right a wrong—and that's all we wanted. You had no interest in the commandership itself, not the power and glory that comes with it, just killing Chris. Nothing else. It was refreshing to see someone with the same desire as us."

"We had our doubts," Darius said. "How well could someone so new truly do in this type of role? But the role didn't matter; you only leveraged it to get us to this moment of victory. Even the Council wanted to stop this, but you pressed forward. Not to mention, we were all aware of the romance between you and Sonya. For me personally, I knew the moment you agreed to kill her that we had this in the bag. I suppose every commander had their share of obstacles, as Marie mentioned, but yours were personal. You came to terms with them on your own, and that cleared the path. Commander Briar, I hope you don't take this the wrong way—because we all know the kind of man you are—but you are the best commander in the history of the organization."

Tears welled in Martin's eyes as he listened. He looked to

Arielle for assurance, and she only returned a nod and grin. Darius finally released his grip on Martin's hand, taking a step back and shaking his head while he looked at Chris on the ground.

"I'm not sure what to say . . . thank you." Martin wiped his tears away, feeling them on the verge of freezing over his eyeballs.

"Nothing to say, Commander," Darius said. "Job well done. Now, are we ready to get this dead bastard out of here and back to Winnipeg?"

"I thought you'd never ask," Arielle chuckled.

The four of them each grabbed a limb, hoisting Chris into the air, the limp body not weighing very much thanks to his sudden aging that had caught up with him in his final days. As always, he wore his signature black suit, and Martin brushed his fingers along the pants, sensing the memories and destruction that had once swarmed within the man. He thought back to the day he and his mother entered Wealth of Time, neither aware what that one simple visit would lead to.

They trudged through the woods, moving at an excited pace, all three of them anxious—and honored—to hear the story firsthand from their commander of how he finally killed Chris Speidel. The story would take its own form in the coming months as people added little details and bent the story to make it dramatic in their own way. But these four would forever know exactly how it all played out.

Chapter 30

Martin and the crew arrived back to the jet in Winnipeg to a raucous welcome party. He had placed the phone calls he wanted once they arrived back to the vehicles in Angle Inlet, receiving a deafening howl from Steffan all the way in England. His call with Alina turned into an emotional conversation that she promptly ended, wanting to wait until they were together in person.

Darius and Marie drove the van with Chris's body, Martin and Arielle trailing behind for the entire trip back. The car ride was a completely different scene compared to their trip out of Winnipeg. Music blared and laughter filled the vehicle. Martin and Arielle swapped stories of their early lives, mainly the good memories.

By the time they arrived to the jet, it was close to one o'clock in the morning. Everyone was wide awake, lining up in two opposite rows to form a pathway for Martin and everyone else to file back up the stairs, and onto the jet where a full dinner spread had been catered, and the bar had been restocked.

A round of applause greeted them for a solid two minutes, each individual team member taking the opportunity to either shake Martin's hand or give him a big hug as he made his way through the tunnel of people. Every face he saw had been on this mission since its first days. He'd seen these people through ups and downs in the matter of a few weeks, but nothing could replace the sheer glee now stuck on their faces.

A stretcher was brought out to help carry Chris's body onto the jet, a handful of members volunteering to do the honors while everyone else gawked in disbelief at the dead body of a man who had at one point ruined their lives.

Martin led the procession up the stairs, where Alina waited at the top with a generous grin.

"Welcome back, Commander," she said, opening her arms to hug him. She planted a kiss on his cheek before whispering in his ear. "Thank you."

"It's great seeing you," Martin said. "Can't say I thought I'd actually be back here." He looked around the jet as if he had marooned on a foreign island. All chairs and tables had been pushed along the edges of the cabin to clear room for an open floor. A solid black sheet hung from the ceiling where Martin's seat was normally stationed, a podium set up in front of it.

Alina followed his gaze. "We're ready for your big speech. Did you prepare any remarks? Do you want to get changed out of those bloody clothes? You look like you got mauled by a bear."

"Let the people see the fruit of my work. I haven't prepared anything on paper, but I have been thinking over what I want to say. You don't think we should wait until the morning? How many people are honestly going to watch this right now?"

"A lot has been put in motion since you left. I opened a line of communication with Uribe, and once I got word from you, he lifted the blackout and informed all members to be ready for a special announcement likely to come in the middle of the night. I'm sure the rumors are flying, but our protesters have retreated, leaving just the Revolters out on the streets to get scooped up by local authorities. At this point, people are assuming that you're either dead or have pulled off the impossible. Both circumstances are hard for everyone to process."

"Well then, I guess they're gonna be pleased to see me."

"We're ready when you are."

"Let's do this."

The rest of the team had made their way onto the jet, two members sliding a table behind the podium where they would lay the stretcher holding Chris. The noise level immediately rose as chatter filled the confined space, an impromptu—and deserved—party breaking out.

Alina put two fingers between her lips and whistled, a piercing sound that dropped a hammer on all the noise. "I know we are all very excited to party the night away, but our work is not done. Commander Briar needs to deliver a speech to the organization, then a small team of us will need to make preparations for disposing of Chris's body. Commander Briar is ready, so we'd appreciate your undivided attention. And yes, you can cheer if the speech calls for it."

Martin made his way to the podium, stealing a quick glance at the dead body that would decorate the background behind him. He faced the camera and nodded, the camera operator counting down with his fingers until pointing at Martin, surely the biggest audience to have ever tuned in to an organizational address.

"Good morning, Road Runners," Martin said with a smirk. "I want to first apologize for surely getting most of you out of bed at such a late hour, but monumental events cannot wait to be announced. I also want to apologize for the stress I have caused the organization over the past few weeks. I have been absent from my office and regular duties to work on this weeks-long mission. It is my great pleasure to announce that the mission is complete."

The small crowd on the jet erupted in applause. The TVs in the jet showed the live stream, and Martin noticed the camera view showed Martin off-center to the right of the screen, strategically allowing the viewers at home to see Chris Speidel, from the stomach up, on the left-hand side.

"As you can see behind me, Chris Speidel is dead."

Martin paused, allowing a moment for the news to sink in for all those watching around the world. The cell phone in his pocket immediately started buzzing and would remain in that state for the next two hours. His team on the jet hollered and shouted, hugging each other now that the announcement had been officially made. Their commotion rumbled the jet to the point of making Martin wonder if they were getting ready for takeoff. The celebration carried on for five minutes, Martin remaining behind the podium, smiling and nodding to both the camera and those in front of him, thanking everyone for their showering of joy. The moment grew somewhat awkward for Martin, feeling stuck behind the podium while the entire Road Runner world lost their minds. He wasn't even halfway through his speech that had now been put on pause. Once the applause finally died down, Martin continued.

"I want to award a major token of gratitude to this team here with me. Every single person here has been working around the clock for nearly a month. No one has had a full night's sleep during this mission, and many have been on the road with no contact to their family and friends. Thank you all for the sacrifices you have made to make this possible."

Martin paused and took a sip of water while another round of applause went around. He looked forward to getting drunk off whiskey and falling asleep at the next opportunity he could.

"I also need to take a moment to thank Sonya Griffiths. Without going into details, Sonya decided to sacrifice her life to make this mission possible. As you may know, Chris had injected his blood into her system when she was a child, guaranteeing him a life of invincibility as long as she lived. Without her sacrifice, this mission would have surely hit multiple road blocks along the way, and may have ended up failing. I know that Sonya had a rocky ending to her relationship with the Road Runners, but if I can forgive her, then so should you.

"I understand the shock you might be experiencing from hearing this news today—you may even have doubts that Chris is really dead. I understand the concerns, and that is why our plans for his remains will include dismembering his body into thirteen different parts. The parts will be sealed in steel boxes to either be buried in a remote location, or dumped into the ocean. We will keep one of the sealed boxes in the Road Runners' headquarters, and it will transfer to wherever our next commander chooses to base the headquarters during their term.

"The day has come for us to no longer live in fear. When the sun rises later this morning, rest assured that it is rising not only over a new day, but also a new era for the Road Runners. We've lost so many of our own during the past several months in what ended up being a bloody end to this war. Let's take the time to mourn those losses, but also keep our heads up. We can operate without the lingering threat of destruction. We can walk down the streets again with our friends and families and not have to constantly look over our shoulders. We can even start building our offices above ground, and live our lives free of worry.

"I came into this position reluctantly. I had no experience, and honestly no desire, to be the commander for all of you fine members. All I had was an unrelenting need to kill Chris Speidel. Now, as I look to our future, I can't help but to be filled with pride of what we have accomplished and what still lies ahead. This organization was founded to counter the antics of the Revolution, and we have seen that purpose through. We now have the unique opportunity to shape our organization into whatever we want it to be for the long-term future. I'll be relying on you, the members, to help form this new vision. Let's take our time and seriously consider what we want that future to look like. This team by my side will be taking a much-deserved vacation as soon as we handle Chris's remains—it's an order. And once they're all back, I'll also take a brief break to clear my head. During that time, I encourage you all to have conversations with each other, discuss what you like about our existing structure, and, more importantly, what you don't like. We will set up a system for the millions of you to deliver your remarks so that myself and the Council can review and implement changes the majority wants.

"Until then, be proud of what we have accomplished. I look forward to returning to the normal day-to-day we were once accustomed to. Good night, and may you each have the brightest future imaginable."

Martin nodded to the camera and stepped away once he received the okay that the feed had been cut. Those on the jet offered one final round of applause before someone turned on the radio, blaring "We Are the Champions" to kick off the not-so-subtle celebration.

Martin went to the bar where a drink had already been poured for him, and he watched his team commemorate the grandest achievement of their lives. Never could he recall seeing so much joy in one room. He saw Alina and Arielle across the way, knowing the bright futures ahead for both.

They all had one, Martin included, and the thought brought a smile to his lips as his thirty seconds of alone time were up. He'd be in and out of different conversations until they landed in Denver in the wee hours of the morning.

Chapter 31

Two days later Martin sat in his office, enjoying the lack of constant commotion as he stared at his computer screen, a never-ending list of emails that he attempted to sort through. They had piled up over the weeks he was missing from the public, resulting in the earlier emails to contain cries for his appearance, some worried, some enraged, while the later ones were nothing but congratulatory messages.

He had been hard at work since they arrived back to Denver, first fielding a heated call from the rest of the commanders. His choice to utilize a foreign member to freeze time was a major violation to their Bylaws, punishable by removal from the commandership, but Commander Blair surprisingly served as the voice of reason, citing the time of peace that now graced North America for the first time in the Road Runners' existence. They let him off the hook, choosing to focus on what their futures held instead of falling into a political fight with no obvious end result.

After the phone call, Martin headed for the conference room next door, where a mortician and orthopedic surgeon had set up shop for the separation of Chris's body. It had been a gruesome process to watch, spanning over six hours as they broke the body into thirteen different parts. He watched as the body parts, intentionally severed mid-limb, were packed into different six-cubic-feet steel safes, the locks promptly damaged as soon as they were sealed shut, ensuring no one could ever crack them open.

Multiple crews waited on standby, each ready to take a box to a different part of the continent. Some were dropping them in the oceans, others to be buried in secret islands in the Caribbean, but one in particular was to remain in the Denver office, and that's what Martin waited for behind his desk today, after the conference room had been cleared out and restored to its regular function.

The knock came on the door, Alina entering with the solid black safe in her embrace. "Good morning, Commander, I take it you heard the body has now been successfully distributed to all of our target locations?"

"Sure did—it's still taking time to feel real, you know?"

"Absolutely. I never realized how conditioned I was to constantly be waiting for bad news to break. Now, it kind of feels like vacation."

Martin chuckled. "Wait until your *actual* vacation. You all packed for that?"

"Commander, I packed the night we arrived home from Winnipeg. Two days away from Hawaii—I can already taste that first Mai Tai on the beach."

"Good for you. Is that what I think it is?" he asked, nodding to the box.

"Yes—here is the head of Chris Speidel, forever locked in this safe, and to stay within the office of the commander for as long as we exist."

She stepped forward and placed it on the front of his desk. Martin stared at it, both amused and disturbed by the thought of what lay inside. *A human head,* he thought. *That's some mafia shit.*

"Honestly, Commander, I don't think anyone would care if you held on to this, even beyond your term. You've earned it, and it's very much yours."

Martin raised his hand. "This is official property of the Road Runners. Maybe I'll take other mementos when my term comes to an end, but this needs to stay right here where it belongs, to forever serve as a reminder of what we had to go through."

Alina nodded. "Are you about ready to head out?"

"Absolutely." Martin grabbed a light jacket and pulled it on. He had wanted to visit the gravesites of Izzy and Sonya, buried next to each other at the cemetery in Larkwood, as Martin had instructed. Alina volunteered to drive, knowing it would be an emotional event for Martin.

They climbed the steps to the marketing office above, passing through and stepping outside to a world that smothered them with unlimited freedom. In a matter of two days, nearly all the Revolution had gone under the radar. Homes of known Revolters were checked, and no one ever answered. A good amount were also in local prisons thanks to their public attacks in the days leading up to Chris's death. Martin had expected as much, just not so soon. He still had security guards whenever he stepped outside, only they didn't cling to his every move. For this trip, they would follow behind in a vehicle of their own, and would remain about fifty yards back once at the cemetery.

Martin got into the passenger seat of Alina's BMW, and sunk back as they pulled onto the road, weaving through the familiar traffic of downtown Denver. Alina had punched their destination into the GPS that predicted the trip would take fifteen minutes.

They rode in silence until reaching the freeway, Martin gazing out the window. When they had passed the Sixteenth Street Mall, he imagined the ghosts of the life he once had, Lela and Izzy leaving him behind at work, never having to worry about a gunman opening fire right next to them. He thought of collecting his fortune after arriving back from his first time travel trip, he and Sonya planning a life together that had been nothing but a game for her. The pain of the past always fades, but its scars remain forever, a reminder of what had been endured.

When they reached the outskirts of downtown, headed north to Larkwood, Alina broke the silence. "We found something you need to know about."

Martin sensed the shift in her tone, causing him to squirm in his seat. "What is it?"

"Well, as you know, we've been going through all of Chris's property, just rummaging for whatever we might find, and we've struck something that is both powerful and dangerous. At first we came across a book—it seemed odd at first, considering Chris had no other books with his possessions. It's called the Book of Time, and it contains all the secrets from the past Keepers of Time: their special abilities, how to use them, rituals, initiation processes, pretty much everything you can imagine."

"Are you kidding me?!" Martin gasped. "Is the recipe for creating Juice in there?"

"It sure is."

"Holy shit—this is life-changing."

"Let's not get ahead of ourselves. I am having the book delivered to the office later today. We'll have to look through it and decide what we want to do. But there's more to it. The book was one thing, but we found an actual *vial* of liquid that we are certain transforms a person into the Keeper of Time. Based on the brief reading of that particular section of the book, it all lines up."

Martin let out a nervous laugh. "Well, that's something we need to dump down the drain. If it exists, there will always be a possibility of another Chris rising to power."

"But Commander, it's in *our* possession. We can handle it responsibly. I think you'll want to read through this book before making any final decision on it."

"And is this coming with the book? How do we know someone hasn't already drank it themselves and is preparing to conquer the world?"

"The transformation process is . . . brutal. And it takes forty-eight hours to complete. The vial will come with the book tonight."

"Look, there is no reason for a single person to hold that much power. I'm not interested, and neither should you be. I'll keep an open mind and will read this book, but don't count on me becoming the Keeper of Time."

"I understand, Commander, and even agree. But it appears there are some things we can make happen. Multiple Keepers, replication of the fluid, and lots of good that can come with these special abilities. I look forward to discussing it all in more detail once we have the book."

Martin leaned against his window, staring out as they turned into the cemetery. That this all existed seemed like one final way Chris had left his legacy behind, one final thing to cause stress for Martin Briar. Would he truly be able to live in peace? Or was this going to set up a new, fresh list of worries?

He shook the thoughts from his mind, shifting his focus to

his first visit to Sonya's grave.

The cemetery's inner roads were three connected loops. Alina rounded the first one and stopped toward the back of the second, killing the engine. "Do you want me to come out with you?"

Martin shook his head. "If you don't mind, I'd like to have a word with them in private."

"Of course. I'll be here."

He stepped out of the car, legs wobbly as the nerves assembled throughout his body. He had been here at least two dozen times since they buried Izzy's and Marilyn's remains.

Martin crunched through the few leaves laying scattered across the ground, their earthy stench filling his nose as the hum of passing vehicles from the nearby freeway created a backdrop of steady white noise.

He reached the three graves, straddling the space that separated Izzy and Sonya, his mother to the left of Izzy. He looked to his daughter on the left, Sonya on his right, and shook his head, liquid immediately welling in his eyes. Two minutes passed as Martin stood in silence, letting the tears stream down his face, their salty flavor seeping into his mouth through pursed lips.

"Never in my life would I have imagined seeing both of you buried underground, let alone next to each other. Izzy, you were always the sparkling light I needed to get through the dark days that followed your disappearance. Just the thought of you could turn my day around. You'll never understand how much I loved you. I came into this whole mess just to see you—to *save* you. I failed that particular mission, but I learned so much about myself during that time. Even in death, you still brought light to my life. And I'll never forget how you came to see me in the woods, at a time when I truly thought my life was minutes away from ending. You gave me everything I needed that night."

Martin sniffled and wiped away the tears and mucus that had pooled on his chin and nose, turning his attention to Sonya, her big-lettered GRIFFITHS not having an obvious affiliation to Izzy Briar next door, their connection being Martin's own secret. He had considered having her remains laid to rest in Colorado Springs, next to her mother, but figured since he was the last person alive who actually loved her, that it would be better if she was closer for him to visit.

"And you, Sonya," he said, a small grin forming. "I can't say our love story was one to ever be made into a movie—I'm not even sure what it was. I loved you, that's all I know, and that's all that mattered to me. I know the feelings were there. And the way it all ended only confirms that your love may have been even stronger than I thought. I know what you did wasn't for your father—it was for me. For all of us. I'll forever cherish the time we had, and will always wonder what could have been. And you'd better know that I'll always defend your name when it comes up in conversation—you're the one who made all of this possible. I'll never forget you, and can't wait until the day we cross paths again."

He shuffled to his left, standing over his mother's grave. "Mom, I don't even know where to start. Thank you for everything. I doubt you knew any of this would unfold by our simple visit to that antique store, but it has changed me for the better. I never thought I'd be able to conquer the mountain of grief following Izzy's death, but this has shown me a new life. One with hope and happiness. Purpose. I don't know how it all happened, but you saved my life with the message you relayed through Izzy that day in the woods. I love you, and will always work to make you proud."

Martin stood there a moment longer, savoring the nostalgia that ran through his head, dreading the thought of having to return to his new life as a commander of peace. He only wanted to sit in the cemetery all day and carry on these conversations with the muted gravestones.

Your term isn't forever—there will be plenty of time for that.

While Martin understood this, his perception of time since joining this secret universe had been pure confusion. It had only been two years since he took that initial pill in the Wealth of Time store, but everything that had happened since made it feel like a decade. In the grand scheme of things, his two-year term was sure to fly by, soon to be another memory that he'd reflect back as a life-changing event.

For now, he dropped to a knee and kissed each of his hands, planting them on the grass that grew above the women who had reshaped his mid-life and beyond. With one final wipe of the tears, Martin Briar rose to his feet and returned to the car where not just Alina waited, but the road to a hopeful future ahead. As they drove off, Martin leaned his head against the window, staring to the graves, knowing the hardest part of his commandership—and his life—were now behind him, promising to never let anything threaten what he had accomplished.

I will never let any of you down.

GET EXCLUSIVE BONUS STORIES!

Connecting with readers is the best part of this job. Releasing a book into the world is a truly frightening moment every time it happens! Hearing your feedback, whether good or bad, goes a long in shaping future projects and helping me grow as a writer. I also like to take readers behind the scenes on occasion and share what is happening in my wild world of writing. If you're interested, please consider joining my mailing list. If you do so, I'll send you the following as a thank you:

1. A free copy of *Revolution*, a prequel story that goes back in time before Chris Speidel ever knew about the mysterious world of time travel.
2. A free copy of *Road Runners*, a prequel story that visits the origination of the Road Runners organization.

You can get your content **for free,** by signing up HERE.
https://www.andregonzalez.net/Wealth-Of-Time-Bonus

Acknowledgements

It's hard to believe this series has ended. When I first started, I didn't have a plan for how many books it would run, but as I finished Keeper of Time, the fourth book, I felt two more were enough to complete Martin's story. Even though I have worked on some other projects during this series run, the prior three years have felt entirely dedicated to the Wealth of Time series. I suppose I'll always look back to the time frame of March 2018-May 2021 as the time I grew and learned the most as an author.

Writing a trilogy, which I've done three, is simpler to structure out the series. Writing a fourth book and beyond, however, is an entirely different beast. It takes a particular dedication to keep the story-line fresh and moving forward (but not too fast!). As the author, the characters can become repetitive once you've drilled into as much of their backstory as you can find. It's strenuous work, but rewarding to reach this point.

With every ending comes a new beginning. I have some ideas lined up for life after Wealth of Time, and I hope you'll stay with me on this journey.

Before we turn the page, however, I need to thank those who have helped make this series a possibility. First is my editor, Stephanie Cohen-Perez. Our first project happened to be the first book of this series, and there has been no looking back. Readers may not understand just how much an editor contributes to make the book a cleaner reading experience. My success is your success, and I hope you take equal pride in this Wealth of Time universe as me.

People say to not judge a book by its cover, but that is precisely what we do as readers. Thank you to Dane Low for having the perfect vision for this series. I can't envision these covers any other way.

Writing can be a lonely gig, and it's important to have friends who understand the grind and struggle. Thank you to the Dizzy Dragons for being there every step of the way.

Thank you to Arielle. A seemingly ordinary moment we shared sparked the premise for this entire series. I suppose the extraordinary can happen anytime, and it's important to be ready.

Felix and Selena, don't think you're out of the woods just because Arielle sparked the idea. Similar moments have occurred, and I can't wait to create a new universe where you are all the stars of the show!

Thank you to all of the family, friends, and fans who have supported me. You all make this possible, and I am forever indebted to you.

Lastly, thank you to my wife, Natasha. I could write an entire book on the help you provide, both behind-the-scenes and openly. Whether it's new marketing ideas, or bouncing around new thoughts for stories, you always come through. I couldn't imagine anyone else by my side as we climb this mountain. I love you.

Andre Gonzalez

November 1, 2020 — March 17, 2021

Enjoy this book?

You can make a difference!

Reviews are the most helpful tools in getting new readers for any books. I don't have the financial backing of a New York publishing house and can't afford to blast my book on billboards or bus stops.

(Not yet!)

That said, your honest review can go a long way in helping me reach new readers. If you've enjoyed this book, I'd be forever grateful if you could spend a couple minutes leaving it a review (it can be as short as you like) on the Amazon page. You can jump right to the page by clicking below:

mybook.to/TimeofFate

Thank you so much!

Also by Andre Gonzalez

Wealth of Time Series:
  Time of Fate (Wealth of Time Series, Book #6)
  Zero Hour (Wealth of Time Series, Book #5)
  Keeper of Time (Wealth of Time Series, Book #4)
  Bad Faith (Wealth of Time Series, Book #3)
  Warm Souls (Wealth of Time Series, Book #2)
  Wealth of Time (Wealth of Time Series, Book #1)
  Road Runners (Wealth of Time Series, Short Story)
  Revolution (Wealth of Time Series, Short Story)

Insanity Series:
  The Insanity Series (Books 1-3)
  Replicate (Insanity Series, Book #3)
  The Burden (Insanity Series, Book #2)
  Insanity (Insanity Series, Book #1)
  Erased (Insanity Series, Prequel) (Short Story)

The Exalls Attacks:
  Followed East (#2)
  Followed Home (#1)
  A Poisoned Mind (Short Story)

Standalone books:
  Resurrection (Amelia Doss Series, Book #1)

Snowball: A Christmas Horror Story

About the Author

Born in Denver, CO, Andre Gonzalez has always had a fascination with horror and the supernatural starting at a young age. He spent many nights wide-eyed and awake, his mind racing with the many images of terror he witnessed in books and movies. Ideas of his own morphed out of movies like *Halloween* and books such as *Pet Sematary* by Stephen King. These thoughts eventually made their way to paper, as he always wrote dark stories for school assignments or just for fun. Followed Home is his debut novel based off of a terrifying dream he had many years ago at the age of 12. His reading and writing of horror stories evolved into a pursuit of a career as an author, where Andre hopes to keep others awake at night with his frightening tales. The world we live in today is filled with horror stories, and he looks forward to capturing the raw emotion of these events, twisting them into new tales, and preserving a legacy in between the crisp bindings of novels.

Andre graduated from Metropolitan State University of Denver with a degree in business in 2011. During his free time, he enjoys baseball, poker, golf, and traveling the world with his family. He believes that seeing the world is the only true way to stretch the imagination by experiencing new cultures and meeting new people.

Andre lives in Denver with his wife, Natasha, and their three kids.

Made in the USA
Middletown, DE
22 September 2023